# BEYOND THE PALE

## 5 Arresting Tales of Love & Other Hauntings

By
K. Patrick Malone

# BEYOND THE PALE

## 5 Arresting Tales of Love & Other Hauntings

By
K. Patrick Malone

**Argus Enterprises International, Inc.**
North Carolina***New Jersey

# BEYOND THE PALE
## 5 Arresting Tales of Love & Other Hauntings

A-Argus Better Book
For information:
Argus Enterprises International, Inc.
P O Box 914
Kernersville, NC 27284
www.a-argusbooks.com

ISBN: 978-0-6156964-5-4

**Book Cover by: Dubya**

Printed in the United States of America

# INSIDE A HAUNTED MIND

"*My skin crawls even to write about it,* says Malone's protagonist, Terry Chagford. These words will ring true for all who delve into the mentally unhinging world of small town police chief Chagford in K. Patrick Malone's suspense thriller *Inside a Haunted Mind*...Riveting from the start...one may get so lost in this story that the conclusion comes as somewhat of a shock. One factor that gives this story its tone—almost missed due to its subtleness—is Malone's uncanny ability to portray Chagford's downward spiral toward insanity. It is as if he himself has experienced what it is like to be inside a haunted mind. The book is an excellent work, but only those able to handle graphic descriptions of depraved violence should enter Malone's world of terrifying horror."

*ForeWord Magazine Book Review*

\*~\*

"This is a good, old-fashioned ghost story complete with an old, creepy house, spirits and flying furniture. Or is it? Could it be nothing more than the illusions of a haunted and disturbed mind? The reader will have to pay close attention to figure it out. At times the vividly created characters wrap readers up in their stories and eventually they are all tied to a set of long-ago murders...overall, a good read."

*Chattanooga Times Free Press*

\*~\*

"*Inside a Haunted Mind* is a dark story about a relentless evil force closing in on small town police chief Chagford...a suspense-laden deconstruction of a good man's mind gone terribly wrong, laced with shocking revelations and edge-of-the seat tension."

*Midwest Book Reviews*

# THE DIGGER'S REST

"When people search for proof of the legendary King Arthur, few think to hunt down his skeleton. THE DIGGER'S REST is a story of a team of archaeologists as they dig through the ruins of an ancient medieval castle for the body of Arthur. While they begin to shine a new light on one of history's mysteries, the terrifying discovery isn't the one they were looking for. Adventure blended in a large bit of horror, THE DIGGER'S REST is a solid pick for suspense readers."

*Midwest Book Reviews*

\*~\*

"Outstanding bit of writing sure to keep the reader enthralled until the final unexpected twist....A must for the readers of the *Stephen King* ilk…"

*Mid-Atlantic Reviews*

\*~\*

"Now and then an author comes along who tops each of his preceding work with one that is even better. Malone is already an adult in the realm of the macabre, and continues to grow with this latest chilling novel. THE DIGGER'S REST…Read it if you dare"

Jackson Owensby
*Deliberate Indifference* and
*My Sister and I: We Are Survivors.*

## AN UNFINISHED HOUSE

"…tremendously raw and powerful…Malone seems to be experiencing a growth in the breadth of his expression that again makes his most recent novel a most interesting read."

John H. Manhold,
author of *El Tigre, Lobo*
and *The Elymais Coin*

*~*

"The weight of the world comes at you all at once. *An Unfinished House* is a thriller following a man devastated by the death of his wife and his discovery of a secret surrounding his recently purchased home, leaving him facing a serious challenge of life as he seeks truth. *An Unfinished House* is a riveting read that will prove difficult to put down."

*Midwest Book Reviews*

## THE HOUSE AT MILLER'S COURT

"Also in fiction from K. Patrick Malone is *The House at Miller's Court* as a family copes with the fear of losing their son and the mysteries behind it all, an excellent addition for fans of Malone's work."

*Midwest Book Reviews*

*Inside A Haunted Mind*

****Wild Card Winner, New England Book Festival, 2009****
****Winner, USA Book News National Best Books Awards, 2008****
****Honorable Mention, Paris Book Festival, 2010****
****Honorable Mention, Beach Book Festival, 2010****
****Honorable Mention, San Francisco Book Festival, 2009****
****Honorable Mention, Arizona Author's Association, 2008****
****Honorable Mention, Hollywood Book Festival, 2007****


*The Digger's Rest*

****Winner, Halloween Book Festival 2011****
****Honorable Mention, New England Book Festival, 2009****
****Honorable Mention, New York Book Festival, 2008****
****Honorable Mention, Hollywood Book Festival, 2008****


*An Unfinished House*

****Gold Medal-Horror, National Indie Excellence Book Awards 2010****
****Winner, USA Book News National Best Books Awards, 2010****
**** Winner, Arizona Authors Association (2nd prize), 2010****
****1st Runner-up Winner, New York Book Festival 2009****
****Bronze Medal-Horror, ForeWord Magazine Book of the Year Awards 2010****
****Honorable Mention, Paris Book Festival 2010****
****Honorable Mention, Beach Book Festival, 2010****
****Honorable Mention, New England Book Festival 2009****
****Honorable Mention, Los Angeles Book Festival 2009****
****Honorable Mention, Nashville Book Festival 2009****
****Honorable Mention, London Book Festival 2009****

*The House at Miller's Court*

****Gold Medal-Horror, National Indie Excellence Book Awards 2011****
****Wild Card Winner, Paris Book Festival 2011****
****1st Runner-Up, Los Angeles Book Festival 2011****
****Winner, Arizona Authors Association (2nd prize), 2011****
****Bronze Medal-Horror, ForeWord Magazine Book of the Year Awards 2011****
****Honorable Mention, London Book Festival 2011****
****Honorable Mention, Halloween Book Festival 2011****
****Honorable Mention, New York Book Festival 2010****
****Honorable Mention, Hollywood Book Festival 2010****
****Honorable Mention, Beach Book Festival 2010****

*Beyond The Pale*
*5 Arresting Tales of Love & Other Hauntings*
*(The Short Stories)*

*~*

1st Runner-Up
*"Army Brat"*
Hollywood Book Festival 2012
(Best Unpublished Story)

*~*

1st Runner-Up
*"One Little Indian Boy"*
New York Book Festival 2012
(Best Unpublished Story)

## Acknowledgements

With special thanks to Rona Abramow, John Todd, Mr. Gene Autry & the City of Tombstone, Arizona without whom this collection could not have been imagined. To Luis Merced, for his generosity and intelligence.

KPM

## <u>Dedication</u>

Trisha (Goddess) Moore, my biggest fan, favorite editor and right-hand gal, for all the help you've given me on so many levels.

KPM

# BEYOND THE PALE
## 5 Arresting Tales of Love
## & Other Hauntings

## TABLE OF CONTENTS

# *Tableau Vivant*

**Tableau vivant** (plural: **tableaux vivants**) is French for "*living picture*." The term describes a striking group of suitably costumed actors or artist's models, carefully posed and often theatrically lit. Throughout the duration of the display, the people shown do not speak or move. The approach thus marries the art forms of the stage with those of painting. The most recent heyday of the tableau vivant was the 19th century with virtually nude tableaux vivants or "*poses plastiques*" providing a form of erotic entertainment.

*"All the world's a stage, and all the men and women merely players. They have their exits and their entrances, and one man in his time plays many parts, his acts being seven ages."*

As You Like It- Act 2, scene 7,
139–143, William Shakespeare

*"Heavenly shades of night are falling, it's twilight time.*
*Out of the mist your voice is calling, 'tis twilight time.*
*When purple-colored curtains mark the end of day,*
*I'll hear you, my dear, at twilight time."*

Twilight Time,
The Platters (1958)

# Act I

## Enter Rena Sokol

*(Actress enters dark stage from left, crosses to stage right and sits in a window seat overlooking the street. Light appears, stage light comes up to reveal an upper middle-class New York apartment.)*

Sitting in the window seat, she watched the sun rise over the Manhattan horizon through the picture window of her father's apartment; the purple-gray sky giving way to the underlying sliver of warm light as the sun crept to life little by little. She took a deep breath then rose to refill her coffee cup. On the way back to her place by the window, she stopped, reached into her bag and pulled out a small square pack, gold and white; Marlboro Lights, a small lighter with it in her hand.

When she got back to the window, she seated herself comfortably, pulling her white plush terrycloth robe down over her bare thighs and calves as she curled her feet beneath her. She lit a cigarette from the pack, keeping her eyes on the ever-growing light of the new day.

Sunday…it was Sunday, always the loneliest day for Rena Sokol, and even lonelier in the last six weeks. She hadn't been alone in the apartment for so long, only from the time her father went into the hospital, and now for good. It was hers now, for good. She would have never smoked in the apartment if her father had still been alive. It gave her pause for another wave of grief and she wept silently. She did that a great deal lately, going over in her mind all the things her very religious Jewish father would never have tolerated, much less approved of; the things she did anyway, occasional smoking, occasional drinking, and worst of all, the fact that never in her life as a woman had she in the least been attracted to the kind of man that her father would have called a good Jewish husband. She liked them big, non-Jewish, working class and, God help her father's memory, very Viking--Aryan looking; blonde or red haired, blue eyes or green. They were all Brians or Michaels, Mitchells or Terrences, Keiths or Kevins, the most common Christian boys names; construction workers, policemen, landscapers. She couldn't help it. They made her crazy. Her father would have lost his mind if he had known, but it was not like she could have ever married them anyway.

Rena Sokol was the only child born of Isaac Sokol, a Jewish immigrant and concentration camp survivor. Her father had been fifty-seven-years old when she was born in 1967. He had already been married with a wife and two children when the war started but he was the only survivor of his family to come to America. Her mother was not young either, thirty-five when Rena was born, an arranged marriage to help heal Isaac Sokol from his losses and give him a reason to live.

For her mother's part, she was a kind, large woman, a good cook and a loving mother. It gave her life purpose to help bring Isaac back into the world of the living. It didn't hurt that Mamie Sokol's father was an increasingly successful garment merchant in Midtown and that he welcomed Isaac into his family and business with open arms. For that, Isaac proved to be a dutiful husband, grew to love his wife, worked hard to make her happy and became successful himself beyond anything he could have imagined. They had a quiet, comfortable life, and as their fortunes grew, no one knew it but them.

As she sat in her window seat, lost somewhere between reality and memory, Rena felt like she could almost hear her father's voice calling to her from his bedroom as he'd done so very many times in their years together, "Renala!" She turned her head instinctively, only catching herself as she remembered that he was gone, a melancholy look washing over her face but one that no one was there to see.

She'd looked after him all of her adult life, living with him, caring for him, listening and learning everything he had to teach her about her family, the history of their people in Europe in both religious and historical terms.

"Why don't you get married, my Renala? Who will look after you when I'm gone?" he'd ask her with his thick Yiddish German accent.

"Please don't talk like that, Papa. And besides, things are different for women these days. I don't need a man to make my life whole," she told him, knowing full well that she was going to be meeting big red-headed and very Catholic Chad for dinner and...later that evening. "And I do have a career, Papa. I'm going to be a famous writer someday...or at least a published one. I don't want to be an English teacher forever, you know."

Isaac Sokol just clapped his hands silently to the air and sighed, looking to the heavens, mumbling something in Yiddish.

When the sun was almost full in the morning sky, Rena got up from the window seat and went into her bathroom. She had to pull herself together enough to meet Gloria for brunch and she hadn't looked at her emails all weekend. Life still had to go on.

In the bathroom, she looked discriminatingly at herself in the mirror, toying with her hair, dark, almost but not quite black, longer than shoulder length and naturally straight, her heart-shaped face showing very few signs of the wear that plagued other women her age, a husband or two, a child or two. It was because she'd stayed unmarried and childless that her alabaster skin had stayed firm and clear, and her features had stayed small; a tiny straight nose, pink sweetheart bow-shaped lips, eyes almost as dark as her hair.

She touched her face as she looked in the mirror, pulling back the skin around her eyes, still a little puffy from her on-again-off-again bouts with grief over the last few weeks, and was suddenly strangely reminded of one of the best compliments a man had ever given her. He was a great big lumberman from the Home Depot over by Gloria's apartment in Brooklyn with a full-sleeve tattoo. She'd gone over with Gloria to help her pick out a door. Gloria left buying a door, but Rena had left with his phone number and his words in a sotto voce telling her that she had, "...*a face like a Hebrew Madonna, a Mona Lisa of Galilee.*" She smiled a small self-conscious smile.

She called him later that afternoon and they had a passionate encounter that evening at his place. He was an art lover, art books, prints and sketches everywhere. It all made sense to her when she saw them and she loved it. He was an artist, too, and from the look in his eyes when she left, she knew that he would draw her. Another faint smile to herself in the mirror as she stepped into the shower to begin the daily ritual that helped keep her that way for as long as possible, "*a Hebrew Madonna, a Mona Lisa of Galilee, huh?*" she thought to herself, "*Maybe so, but you're still almost forty-three.*"

She'd just about finished putting on her daytime makeup when the phone rang in the other room. She rushed to grab it. It could only be one person, Gloria, reminding her of their date and needing to choose a place to meet. Her white terry robe on again, she grabbed the phone on the third ring, just before the voicemail would have picked up. She'd have to remember to change that to five rings; the urgency to rush for anything had left her the day her father died. There was nothing for her to rush for or to anymore.

She heard Gloria Annuzzio's high pitched nasal voice on the other end, full tilt with a Brooklyn accent. Yes, she'd remembered their date, and no, it didn't matter where they ate. Downtown was fine. Yes, the Three of Cups over on First Avenue and East Sixth Street would be fine. No, she wasn't still moping around the house (big lie). Yes, she had thought about what they'd talked about the last time they were out. No she hadn't decided if she wanted to join E-harmony or not. They could talk about it more over brunch.

Gloria had been her best friend since they both started teaching over fifteen years ago. They were both native New Yorkers with their own cultural bents. Rena just listened as Gloria ranted on and on about the benefits of marriage, comfort, security and the ever dwindling possibility of children if she hurried.

The din of Gloria's voice faded into the background as Rena saw the computer over on her desk in the corner of the room. *Damn!* She still had to get dressed and check her emails before she headed out, so the rest of Gloria's lecture on how nice it could be to have the same pair of feet to rub against under the covers every night and how she'd learn to ignore the snoring after a while would have to wait until she got herself downtown. After all, who would know better than Gloria, thrice married, divorced twice, widowed once. "Glory, please honey. If I don't get out of here, I'll never get down there to meet you. You're making me late to meet YOU!" Rena laughed indulgently. Another sharp squawk through the receiver and Rena hung up.

She went over to her computer and turned it on. She didn't expect to find much, a few more condolence messages from friends at work, distant relatives of her mother's from across the country maybe. As soon as she was online, she hit her *read mail* button and the screen frame popped up. She was right. She recognized a number of the screen names of her other friends at work, some even from former colleagues. It started to make her depressed. She hated responding to them, not really knowing what to say. Her father had been ninety-nine years old when he died. She had loved him dearly and would miss him every day, and even though she was adult enough to accept his death as part of the natural process of life, the little girl in her could still see him so clearly in her mind's eye, still hear his voice the way she did when she was growing up, and that's when she would cry. "Damn! Damn! Damn!" she said to herself, grabbing a tissue from the Kleenex box next to the monitor to dab her eyes.

Rena forced herself to think about the life ahead of her and her rash decision to rent her father's apartment out and move downtown. Caught in the emotionalism of the time, she'd gotten the Bohemian bug and had taken a small basement apartment on the Lower East Side in the hopes of living the last of her dreams; writing a novel. She wasn't concerned about commercial success. Her father had left her extremely well off, so well off, in fact, that she never had to work again if she didn't want to. That gave her some comfort and security, but what she wanted most was critical success, to be recognized for her talent and her...message.

She let her mind drift there again, away from the funeral, and the sick bed of her father's apartment to her cramped little brick-walled basement on Cherry Street, and the first time she saw it. She was standing on the sidewalk close to the curb when she first heard the sound, now so real in her mind. She heard the sound again, this time like it was coming from above her head. She looked around. Her eyes landed on a single, lighted window on the second floor of the next building about thirty feet away. A very frail old man, almost mummified with age, was leaning on the window sill with the window half opened staring at her. His stare unsettled her as she watched his trembling hand haltingly rise again to tap on the glass. She could see his lips moving, forming words, unintelligible but seeming as if he was saying, *it weeps.*

"So do I," Rena said to herself sadly, wiping her damp cheeks again. She heard the loud sound of the buzzer and she jumped. *Oh my God! The moving men!* She'd forgotten all about it, and with the holidays so close, she couldn't afford to dally. Gloria would have to wait or come over and help. She was up and at the buzzer in a panic.

"Yes?"

"Move it or Lose it Van Service for Rena Sokol," a gruff voice came back through the microphoned box on the wall. *Be strong, Rena. You can do this,* she thought in a flurry of anxiety then heard a voice from her past come to her aid and in the back of her mind saw her old babysitter Fidelia's face, dark and round. She was a little girl again and had eaten too much sugar. Fidelia was shaking her head and smiling with fond exasperation. Rena could hear her voice so clearly again, *"Chil' dun los' huh mahnd, Mistah Isaac."*

# Act II

## *Enter John Andrew Hill*

*(Lights up. A street scene leading to a store front. Actor [fair haired] enters, arms laden with grocery bags. He walks slowly to the door of the store front, fumbles with the lock then enters. Stage revolves exposing the rest of the store. Actor sets bags down on counter then stops, slowly lowering his head and raising his hands to meet it. Despair. Stop movement. Lights dim.)*

John Andrew Hill brought down the hands that had just splashed cold water on his face and reached for the towel from the towel bar, dabbing it dry. A moment later he was looking in the mirror over the sink. He hadn't really looked at himself in a few years, not really looked *at* himself, only just enough to robotically make sure his trademark clean-cut appearance was just right. It had to be just right, always; a small measure of control in a life where he had very little control. Close-clipped blond hair cut to make the most of the thinning top, a little gel at the front to make it stand out, giving a youthful, almost kewpie doll look to his otherwise rugged, ruddy complexion; dark blue eyes set deeply into a serious brow. But he was looking at himself just then, Christmas Eve, and alone again.

His mind shouted out the question before he could stop it. *Why couldn't they love me?* And his heart started to bleed, just a small hemorrhage to celebrate his forty-eighth Christmas alone…again. But he had to put on a good face for the store. All of the people who had worked so hard with him to fight off not one but two takeover bids for his family-owned hardware and lumber store; the only one on the Lower East Side that mattered since his great-grandfather had started it as an immigrant, having come down to him years later because none of his brothers or sisters wanted it.

They had their families and lives, five of them spread out all over the country from California (his oldest brother) to Florida (his youngest sister) with another brother and sister spread out in-between; doctors, lawyers, teachers; stable, domestic, settled lives. So when his father died three years earlier right at the same time that his second wife told him she was leaving him, he quit his job as a construction manager for a Chicago commercial builder and moved back to New York to take over the store.

As he moved away from the mirror to his closet, he got lost in himself thinking about all the things he'd been avoiding; twice divorced, middle-aged with a comfort paunch around his waist that was, in the end, no real comfort at all. He put on his well ironed khakis and pulled out a crisp, button-down collar shirt; light blue, medium starch and wrinkle free to go over his white crew-neck tee shirt. It was his look, was always his look; 1960s matinee idol like a middle-aged Troy Donahue or Tab Hunter from a Sandra Dee romance or Gidget beach movie.

He went to button his pants and felt that they were just a little tighter around the waist, "Damn!" Food was his comfort and had become increasingly so since he had realized that his second marriage was in trouble. *Is it me? Am I that unlovable?* Then he answered his own thoughts, disgusted with himself. *You're forty-fucking-eight-years old, what the hell difference does it make anymore?*

Back in the bathroom again, he had to check himself in the mirror one more time before he left. There, looking deeply into his eyes, he remembered the beginnings of both relationships; how while they were dating, each of his future wives had made some reference to him looking like Nick Nolte and how important it had been to him then to hear that and feel that maybe he was a little handsome in their eyes. His face got red and his eyes filled, watching in the mirror. *I tried so hard. Why couldn't they love me?*

"Pull yourself together, man," he said bitterly to himself and headed toward the hall of his small apartment. He still had to go out and pick up the orders for the party.

As his father before him had done, and his grandfather before him, he was closing the store early and giving his people a party. It was his turn as the next generation of Hill men to play Fezziwig to the thirty-eight employees of Hill's Hardware and Lumber, Est. 1903.

The first year he was nervous, never really ever expecting he would be the son to stand in his father's shoes. The second year he did it with aplomb, like he really might still be able to pull something meaningful out of this, some semblance of hope still hovering in the back of his mind. Not this year, his third. He would have to struggle this year, but they had all been so good to him since he came back. He couldn't let them down, refused to let them down, especially now since they'd all managed to pull together to keep both The Home Depot *and* Lowe's from taking it away from them. Yes, he owed them, owed them big for their support and loyalty, going the extra mile for him whenever he needed it and prevailing against such enormous odds.

He looked at his watch. "Damn!" He was running late. He threw on his coat and scarf. He had to get a move on, leave the rest behind for a while. Halfway out he stopped, balked and back tracked to the kitchen. He grabbed a large scoop full of cat food from the extra-large bag in the corner of his small Pottery Barn-appointed kitchen and tossed it into the bowl on the floor; two sets of bemused feline eyes watching as he rushed past them, "Sorry, boys. I almost forgot. Don't wait up. I'll be late," and he was out the door, leaving it all behind…for the moment, until later, when he was alone again.

He closed the door behind the last bunch of his people to leave, stumbling and staggering their way toward the street, some hailing cabs; loud cheers and shouts, hugs and tears. "Merry Christmas, John," they shouted back to him as he waved from behind the closed door then pulled the blinds shut. He was alone again.

He surveyed the disaster area that had earlier that evening been the contractor desk of his sales floor and sighed deeply. It was almost unrecognizable; covered with used paper plates, half-filled drink cups, beer bottles, torn down red and green streamers and half deflated red and green balloons. He took a step and heard the crunching sound of broken Christmas balls under his feet from the boys drunkenly challenging each other. "What a mess!" he said to himself aloud, not sure if he was referring to the store or his life in general.

Shaking his head, he strolled slowly around the desk, picking up a plate here, a bottle there, tossing them in the garbage can and taking his time about it. After all, he had nowhere to rush to, no one waiting for him except his cats, Moose and Toby, and he'd left them enough food for the evening.

One by one, he turned off the lights. His feet wandered around aimlessly with plates and cups in his hands, his head seeming to hang lower and lower with each step, moving slower and slower until at last he was alone with only the blinking lights of the Christmas tree. He stopped in the middle of the room and looked around. Memories like ghosts came alive in the shadows created on the walls by the blinking lights; his father and mother, both gone now, his grandfather, gone too, his brothers and sisters when they were kids. He could hear his father's voice shout, *"Brian, keep an eye on John. Don't let him get into anything."* He heard his brother Brian's whining reply, *"Aw Dad. I watched him yesterday. It's Greg's turn today."* His mother's voice, *"Emily, can you pick John up from school today. I have to take Patrick to the doctor for his rash.* He could almost feel Patrick's hands pushing him hard and see his face sticking his tongue out at him, then his grandfather's hands picking him up off the floor and putting him on his lap, smiling as he dusted him off.

Suddenly it seemed that the one great failure of John Andrew Hill's life had come home to him, like a time bomb set to go off just then, at that very moment, taking no prisoners, exploding inside him; a jerking, rending pain followed by a hollow dull ache. He was childless, forty-eight years old and childless; the last of the hardware and lumber Hills to care about any of this. He stood in the center of Hill's Hardware and Lumber, Est. 1903; John Andrew Hill, forty-eight-years old, twice divorced and childless, alone in the dim blinking lights of his Christmas tree and let his face fall into his hands.

When all was done, he wiped his face with some left-over paper napkins and went for his coat and scarf. He could only delay the inevitable for so long. He had to lock up and go home. Slowly, deliberately, he turned the key, shook the knob then walked slowly down the street.

Watching his exhaled breath turn to frozen clouds as they left him, he kicked the fresh snow that had fallen that day like a kid kicking a can down the street. He looked up toward the sky as he meandered down his usual route, turning left on Cherry Street as he had almost every day for the last three years, creature of habit that he was.

The night was quiet. It was after midnight and the world was all warm and comfortable in their homes, maybe in bed, children sound asleep waiting for Santa to come down the chimneys of the row houses and brownstones that lined the sides of the neighborhood street as he passed; peaceful quiet, lonely quiet. Halfway down Cherry Street he stopped for no good reason, just to look at the moon and take a deep breath. He let it out slowly before moving on; a sound, a scream, a woman's voice and a loud crashing noise. It was close, almost right in front of him. He jumped, startled, looking around for the voice. Another crash and another scream. It came from the brownstone on his right, from below.

His eyes shot over just in time to see the basement door of the building come flying open and a woman come running out, frenzied, frantic, long dark hair trailing behind her in the wind. "Help! Someone help me," she cried out breathlessly as she ran directly into him, making a muffled thud sound when they collided. He caught her. She looked up at him, a trickle of blood running down the side of her face from a sharp gash in her scalp; her eyes wild with terror. "There's someone in my apartment, a man, a woman. I don't know; voices, banging, screaming, crying," she cried out to him hysterically, shaking with shock and cold. He stood fast at first, stunned, then came alive, leaving her standing on the sidewalk to call after him as ran into the house. "Be careful!"

A light came on inside, casting a glow on the snow drifting in swirls outside the open door. John Hill came out a few short moments later, hands held out abjectly, a confused look in his dark blue eyes. He saw Rena shivering and pacing maniacally on the sidewalk, her arms wrapped tightly around her, pulling her robe up close around her neck against the freezing winds. She stopped and looked up at him, her eyes still glazed with lingering panic. He went up to her slowly, carefully, and took her by the arm, saying quietly, patiently. "It's clear, Miss. There's no one in there, nothing."

She looked at him, her eyes frantic again, "But I saw them, shadows. He was in my room with her. I saw the shadow of his hands around her throat. She was…struggling and…" she insisted, the pitch of her voice rising in panic again.

John Hill looked at the cut on her head and drew the only logical conclusion. He took her more firmly by the arm and started to guide her back to the door. It was freezing out and she was barefoot. He had to get her inside. "Could it have been a dream, a nightmare maybe?" he asked her delicately, caringly, as he led her back through the door.

She touched her head and felt the trickle of blood that had become sticky from the cold. "A nightmare?" she asked herself out loud. "But it was so real, I saw it. Right there in my living room," she said confused, shaky, an uncertain look in her eyes as she thought about it.

Back in the warm apartment, John Hill led her over to the small futon chair farthest from the door, then went over to the sink and dampened a clean dishtowel. He dabbed the drying stream of blood carefully from her face. "That's quite a knock you've got there," he said. "That must have been some dream," and he smiled at her. She looked up at him, still so unsure.

With her face cleaned and in the light, he saw she was pretty; no makeup, smooth clear skin, a natural serenity in her face so out of place with the confusion still lingering behind her dark eyes. He stopped and walked over to the door. There was a smear of blood still on the edge. She must have opened the door, panicked in the dark, desperate to get out, and slammed her head in a half-sleep dream state before it was fully opened. He looked back to her, "This seems to be the culprit," he said smiling slightly.

"But it seemed so...real. I can still see the shadow on the wall of his hands around her throat," she said, putting her hand up around her own throat and pulling her thick robe closer around it.

He came back over to her and knelt down in front of her. He took her hand, lowering his voice to almost a whisper. "Miss, you really should go to the emergency room. That's a pretty bad gash you've got there. Could probably use a few stitches. Is there somebody I can call for you?" Rena absently felt the increasing lump on her forehead, then got up and went to the bathroom, to the mirror. It *was* a pretty big cut, and deep.

Her head began to swim, her sight narrowed and started to go gray. She heard the loud crash of a glass shattering on the tile floor, echoing as if it were moving somewhere off into the distance. She held onto the sink for support, but there was something else; his hand. He was beside her, holding her up. "I really think we should go, now, Miss. I'll take you myself. We can call anyone you want from the ER, but I really think we should go now," he said, his voice almost a hum in her ear as he tried not to upset her.

He led her back to the chair and sat her down. "Shoes?" he asked. She pointed to a pair of black snow boots over in the corner by the door, just below the coat hooks, and a long black winter overcoat hanging above. He grabbed them both and went back over to her, still dazed on the futon. Down on his knees again, he slowly slipped the snow boots over her little feet, then gently took her arm and helped her stand. He helped her on with her coat, one arm at a time.

With his arm tightly around her, he walked her to the door, feeling so protective of this stranger. He felt her eyes on him.

"I'm Rena," she said, then turned from his glance in embarrassment.

"I'm John," he said quietly, pulling her closer to him as they walked to the curb to look for a cab.

She looked up directly at him then, into his worried eyes. "Do you believe in ghosts, John?" she asked sounding almost like a little girl again, lost and afraid, her dark eyes glazed with a shocked sheen. Stunned by her question, his clever mind thought to himself, *Only the ones we carry with us every day, Rena,* but he spoke differently.

"Nah, ghosts don't scare me. I'm a New Yorker," he said with a goofy, cockeyed smile and pulled her closer, just in time to shore up her weakening knees.


One might have thought that on a Christmas Eve in New York City, the Emergency Room might have been packed full by the ill-conceived activities of the holiday revelers, but the opposite seemed to be true. The reception desk and waiting room at St. Vincent's Hospital Emergency Room seemed uncommonly vacant as they took Rena right into a side examination room, John Hill by her side.

A few moments later the nurse came back with a thin, faded blue hospital gown to exchange for Rena's blood spattered robe. John Hill stood outside while she changed, pacing. He couldn't help it. It just seemed...right. Through the slits in the partition she could see his movements. As she watched his pace widen outside, she found herself strangely comforted by it.

A few seconds later, the nurse drew back the partition and there he was, stopped dead in a half pace; his hands in his pockets. He came back in and sat down next to her. "The doctor will be with you shortly," the nurse said as she left, leaving them alone again.

"Are you sure there isn't someone I can call?" he asked in a low voice, concerned, nervous, looking down at his shoes.

"No, there isn't anyone," Rena said without looking at him, embarrassed beyond imagination, thinking about what a wreck she must look like in front of this strange man; the unforgiving brightness of hospital lights.

The curtain pulled back again and a tall, thin, blonde woman in a white coat walked through. She smiled and put out her hand, "I'm Doctor Petrick," the woman introduced herself with a slight eastern European accent. "Let us take a look at what we have here, shall we?" she said calmly then looked to John Hill just as he was standing to leave. Rena startled out of her daze and looked up at him. The room was so cold, so sterile, reminding her of all the long hours she'd spent in the hospital with her father, then on the day he died, leaving her all alone, and she was afraid. *Please don't leave me alone, John. I'm so afraid*, raced through her head. The doctor looked at Rena. "Your husband?" she asked smiling.

"Yes," Rena said in a spurt, wanting desperately not to be alone at that moment and reached for his hand. He took it, without a thought, or a word, and sat back down, never leaving her side until the stitching was done and she could change back into her own clothes. And even then he went only as far as the other side of the partition.

The keys rattled nervously in her hand as Rena tried to find the keyhole to her front door, her hands still more than a little shaky from the night's trauma. John stood patiently by her side for a moment then gently took the keys from her hand. "Please, let me," he said quietly, a gravelly undertone to his masculine voice.

"It's the big square one," Rena said embarrassed again by her having to fall into a classic caricature of feminine helplessness under stress, turning away from him as she pulled her coat closer around her. He put the key in the lock and turned. The lock clicked open. He turned the knob and pushed.

As the door opened he stood back and waited. Rena went in, turning to him still standing outside the door with his hands in his pockets, his head hanging bashfully down looking at his shoes. He gazed up to look at her. It was the first time she'd really had a chance to look at his face out of her hysteria, as a woman instead of a frightened little girl. He had a brooding, concerned look in his dark blue eyes. "I guess you'll be alright now," he said and moved to walk away, then stopped and pointed at the sky. "The sun should be up soon, nothing to be afraid of anymore," he smiled then turned again to go.

"Wait, John," Rena called out suddenly, a flash in her mind asking her why a Christian man of his age would be out walking alone after midnight on Christmas Eve. Then it dawned on her that he'd never once left her side or her sight all night. He hadn't called anyone to tell them where he was or what he was doing or that he would be late. John Hill stopped in his tracks. "Ya hungry?" she asked, a nervous rush to her words. "It's the least I can do for all you've done for me tonight," she managed to get out before a cold wind rushed past her sending a chill up her spine. She shivered visibly in the doorway.

John came back to the door. "Come on now, you're going to catch your death standing there, to go with that bump on the head," and he smiled slightly, "You've got to be dead on your feet after last night, there's no need to cook for me."

"No, really. I don't mind at all. I've still got all this nervous energy to burn off," she said falling back again into femininity, her long dark hair falling carelessly from behind her ear as she smiled and shook her head, "Oh, I'm so sorry. I completely forgot. It's Christmas Day. You must have a million things to do and your family must be worried sick about you." In that flash of a moment she saw in his eyes that she'd struck a chord. *Clumsy woman*, she thought to herself and tried to rebound, "Please, John, it's the least I can do for your kindness." Another cold wind blew past. She shivered again. It was his primal signal to fall comfortably into his masculinity.

"Oh, alright," he said, smiling an endearingly boyish smile for a man his age. "If it will get you into the house and out of this cold..." and he took a few steps closer like a shy boy kicking at the ground with his foot.

She stepped aside to let him through and closed the door behind them. It was the first time she noticed how tall he was, almost six foot she guessed. She went over to the small kitchenette table and pulled out a chair for him to sit, then began in rush mode, telling him she had to change out of her night clothes and that she'd be out in just a few minutes.

Instead of taking the chair, John stood with his hands in his pockets and looked around the room, noticing the stacked books and papers haphazardly placed on a small table next to a computer station. He walked over slowly and picked up a photograph from a stack of papers. It was old, a sepia-toned picture of a bar-room scene, 1920s, '30s maybe. As he turned to go back to the table something indefinable nagged at him. He couldn't quite put his finger on it. *Something is missing, but what?*

Before he could ponder it further, he heard the door to the other room rattle and saw Rena come into the light of the kitchen area wearing a warm looking, much oversized black turtle neck sweater, man-sized XXL, over a pair of black ski pants and white cotton socks. She had her hair tied back in a ponytail and had put on only the slightest bit of make-up. A cinephile all his life, it couldn't help but draw up in John's mind the image of Audrey Hepburn in the Paris café scene from *Funny Face* and his face began to turn a bright shade of pink from the neck up. He was forty-eight-years old, twice divorced and he was…blushing. She was beautiful. He took a deep breath and sat in the chair she'd pulled out for him earlier.

Rena smiled. "Are you okay?" she asked noticing the sudden change in his color.

"Yeah, fine," he said nodding his head almost comically.

"So what'll it be? I think breakfast would be the most appropriate. Don't you?" she asked as she went over to the apartment-sized refrigerator and opened the door; raising a clatter as she rummaged through it for what she needed.

John nodded. "Sure, that'd be great." He watched in awkward silence as she worked diligently at the stove, turning every so often to put plates on the table, silverware, napkins and coffee mugs. He heard frying as he watched her from behind, and could smell the combined aromas of coffee and of bread toasting. It made him feel warm inside, comforted, and brought to mind the fact that he couldn't remember a time when either of his wives had done that for him in just that way, naturally, seeming almost to enjoy it. She was so different from his wives, both professional working women who seemed to do it only grudgingly to get it done and over with. For the duration of both his marriages, it seemed that if he wanted to get any kind of a decent home-cooked meal that required any care at all, he had to do the cooking himself or go to his mother's while she was still alive.

Suddenly he was pulled out of his thoughts by the muffled thud of a plate in front of him, overflowing with food as it hit the hard wood of the table, eggs over easy with something that resembled bacon, toast, a few small wedges of orange on the side. He looked up to see her smiling at him strangely, something indefinable in her dark eyes as she poured the steaming coffee into his mug. Then she was at the refrigerator and back at the table with her hands full, milk and butter, then back again, with peach preserves and sugar until it was all set before him like…like…he was someone special. He could hardly put words to it, only a wordless concept in his mind. *Home.*

With the small table full with as much as it could hold, Rena sat down opposite him. "Well what are you waiting for? Dig in! You must be starving; a big man like you not having eaten all night," Rena said with a small laugh, all signs of the distress and fear from the night before gone, only the small bandage high on her forehead left to remind him. Her eyes had the shine of finely polished onyx, giving her face a serenity that seemed to be completely at home there.

The smell of the food under his nose, the warmth of the small stove having given the room a cozy feel, he suddenly realized that he was starving and he did as he was told. He dug into the overflowing plate, then stopped, took the napkin from the table and put it in his lap. Rena smiled at that. She liked watching him eat. He had good manners which meant that he had had a good mother. She studied his face as he ate, interrupting only long enough to see if he needed anything. "More toast? More coffee? More…" she refilled his mug, picking slightly at her own plate as she watched him, served him; not being able to keep herself from wondering. She began to study him more…closely. *A sturdy face, as Anglo-Aryan as they come, straight features, finely etched, almost like a sculptor had made him. God? and so…handsome. Wow!* she thought and smiled to herself. *Age? Early forties maybe.*

She noticed his hands as he ate, strong and clean, well worked but scrubbed, fingernails cut close, a smattering of freckles and light blonde hair across the backs. *So…manly.* But something was missing; no wedding ring. *He couldn't be married. No self-respecting wife would ever let a man with a face like his leave the house without his wedding ring.*

In between silent bites, he let his eyes glance up at her, something questioning in his eyes. She felt flushed and she began to fidget nervously around the table, arranging things, wiping around the table. Finally she figured out that he was probably waiting for her; a sign to talk a little.

"What?" she asked curiously.

John Andrew Hill smiled and shrugged, the color coming up around his neck again. "This…bacon sort of stuff is really good but…I don't know what it is." Rena laughed out loud. He didn't know. "It's beef bacon, silly."

In a flash it hit him over the head like a frying pan from her still warm stove; what was missing. He looked around the room again; no Christmas tree or decorations, beef bacon, not pork. She thought she saw the dawning realization in his eyes. It made her uneasy. *Would he be a bigot? A hater?* So she took the comic approach, crossing her eyes and holding her hands up with the affectation of having long fingernails. "So what did ya think? That we all talk like this?" she asked doing her best Barbara Streisand like she did when she and her friends were teenagers. John burst out laughing, his face turning beet red like a little boy who'd just had his first kiss, but his eyes, those penetrating blue eyes peeking out from under that brooding brow, shining away at her; laughing. She felt flushed again; struck by how honest and uncovered they looked. *Can he see me blushing?* Then a voice in the back of her mind, but not Fidelia this time. It made her nervous, very nervous, indeed; more nervous than she'd ever felt in the presence of any man. An electric current ran tingling up her spine. It was Barbara singing…from Funny Girl. *Sadie, Sadie married lady…*

# Act III

## *Duet*

*(Stage Direction: Set is dark, dim light, street scene out front of 81 Cherry Street. A light comes on in the upper side window of the next building. An old man sits in the window behind the light. Light snow begins to fall. Footsteps come from stage right.)*

The snow began to fall lightly as they slowly strolled on their way back from the restaurant. Rena pulled her collar up against the chilly wind. The awkward silence was deafening, but the thoughts darting around their minds were a-chatter, resuming the symphony that had begun that first night in her little kitchenette; a silent symphony...for two, set to the beat of hearts, string instruments finding their harmony...a...duet of thoughts.

| | |
|---|---|
| John: | *She's an upper class, Upper East Side Jewish intellectual, and a writer for God's sake. You are so out of your league, John Andrew Hill.* |
| Rena: | *He makes me feel...safe.* |
| John: | *It felt like home next to her warm stove.* |
| Rena: | *When he looks at me with those eyes, I feel...young again.* |
| John: | *What could she possibly see in me?* |
| Rena: | *He has beautiful hands. What would they feel like...touching me?* |
| John: | *No one like her has ever walked into my life.* |
| Rena: | *I like the way he laughs.* |
| John: | *It feels like she was made just for me.* |
| Rena: | *Lumber and Hardware, huh? I like that. I like it...a lot.* |
| John: | *She makes me feel like a man.* |
| Rena: | *Look at me with those eyes again, John.* |

Before they knew it, they were back in front of the brownstone; so awkward for two grown up people. *Would she ask him in? Does he want to…Should I try to…*a brief stumbling moment as they stood facing each other, each so unsure of what to say, but the symphony was there and they both seemed to find their strings.

Above their heads in the next building, the eyes of the old man watched, just as he had when she first came and again when she met John that night of the trouble. The old man waved his hand to someone on the other side of the room. A woman's hands set an old fashioned boom box on the ledge in front of him. The old man smiled, nodding as John Hill and Rena Sokol stood out front of her apartment, so nervous, neither of them knowing what to do, then the old man hit the button. A familiar sound came out; smooth lyrical… romantic…from the fifties.

*When the twilight is gone, ahhhahhh,*
*and no songbirds are singing, ahhh, ahhh*
*When the twilight is gone, ahhahhh*
*you come into my heart, ahhhahhh….*

John looked up to the source of the music and saw the old man in the window, smiling and holding his frail arms up, one arm high and the other arm coming around as if he were…dancing, and John knew what to do. He held his arms up to Rena like he saw the old man do…

*And here in my heart you will stay…*

She recognized the music on the spot and went into his arms…The Platters.

*…while…I…pray.*

She felt the thick, beefy muscles of his shoulders as she moved her hand up and touched the back of his neck. It felt good, solid…comforting; the skin of his cheek against hers, so warm. *He is a real man.* She closed her eyes and let him lead as they began to turn slowly on the sidewalk outside of 81 Cherry Street; the snow lightly falling obliviously on their heads as they moved.

*My prayer is to linger with you*

*At the end of the day in a dream that's divine.*

First, she smiled. He was a good dancer, better than she might have thought. She liked that.

*My prayer is a rapture in blue*
*With the world far away and your lips close to mine*

*She smells so good,* he thought as he turned his head slightly so his nose could wander just a bit into her hair as they turned around the sidewalk again. It made him feel light-headed being so close to her.

*Tonight while our hearts are aglow*
*Oh tell me the words that I'm longing to know*

She liked the way his hand felt in hers. She opened her eyes and looked; his strong, clean hand holding her smaller one close to his chest, beautiful.

*My prayer and the answer you give*
*May they still be the same for as long as we live*
*That you'll always be there at the end of... my... prayer*

The music stopped and he let her go, stepping back just enough to see her, then another step to feel secure with what he was about to do. He raised his head and looked at her, those penetrating blue eyes fixed on hers, intense and passionate, raw and exposed...lonely, loving, brimming with it...brave and wanting so much to be loved. His lips moved; three words. "Marry me, Rena."

In the fluttering seconds when she saw his lips move and heard his voice, her mind became a riot of echoing voices; her father, *"Why don't you find a nice boy and settle down, Renala?"* Then Gloria, *"The same warm feet under the covers every night, Reen. Trust me. It's a good thing. It's not too late."*

The seconds flickered as she watched his eyes, fixed on hers, so open and waiting. It was right there. She'd found all the reason she needed right in front of her, because in that last second before she spoke, Rena Sokol looked into the eyes of John Andrew Hill, at his face. There was so much there for her to love. She felt like she could swim in it...safe and unafraid. And she knew. For the first time in her almost forty-three-year-old life, she finally knew what it was like. She knew that she could look at that face and into those eyes every day for the rest of her life and never get tired of them, no matter how old they got. *My hero.*

Then the final voice of judgment came rushing up on her from behind, like a sharp slap on the ass, pushing her forward, Fidelia.

"*Chil' dun los' huh mahnd agin, Mistah Isaac!*"

"Yes!"

Later that year, during the week of Thanksgiving, five pairs of hands in places ranging from California and Florida to Michigan and Pennsylvania belonging to Emily Hill Thomas, Brian Hill, Greg Hill, Patrick Hill and Sharon Hill Haggar, respectively, opened small powder blue envelopes, pulling out small matching blue cards and exhibiting various expressions of shock, delight, incredulity and fond laughter; each reading out loud to themselves.

John Andrew Hill and Rena Sokol Hill
Proudly announce the birth of their son,
Micah Isaac Hill, 7 lbs, 9 ounces
on November 2nd @ 3:00am.
The proud parents wish to further welcome you all to attend the bris for Micah Isaac Hill to be held at their new address, 81 Cherry Street, New York, New York, where they fully intend to live...*happily ever after*.
RSVP by December 24th
Accommodations for all attending
will be provided by the proud parents

(Stage Direction: Lights dim to black. Music comes up)

*Sadie, Sadie, married lady that's me!*

**The End**

# ARMY BRAT

***

*"He was just a hired hand, workin' on the dreams he
planned to try, the days go by."*

Tequila Sunrise,
The Eagles (1973)

***

The small rectangular wad started to vibrate in his shirt pocket just as he passed the highway sign reading, *Marana Exit 4 Keep Right*. Keeping one eye on the road, he flipped it open and saw the phone number displayed across the lighted screen. The color came up in his normally pale-skinned neck, now seasoned to the healthy shade of a hearty cut of oak from working most of his adult life in the sun, first turning bright pink, then increasing to crimson as it rushed up his face along with his blood pressure. He hit a button with his finger and held the black plastic wad to his ear. "Don't ever call me again," a steely cold voice came out of his mouth through his clenched teeth and tight lips. "I don't want to hear you. I don't want to see you," he heard his own deep even voice speak into the wad. "You don't exist for me anymore. Do you understand?"

An angry tear came to one of his eyes, threatening to drop any second as he flipped the wad closed violently with a snap. *How could you? How could you do such a thing? Could you really hate me that much?* He took his other hand off the wheel and rolled down the window, then chucked the wad out with a flick of his wrist and a grunt. He watched for only the brief seconds it took to see the small black wad roll end over end on the sun-baked earth alongside I-10 between Phoenix and Tucson.

Joss Meredith used the butt of his hand to wipe away the errant tear, burning as it ran down his face. He then looked in the rearview mirror, first at the increasing distance between him and the last vestige of his…what? *Grief?* Then into his own dark blue eyes set deeply below a strong brow that had three long ridge lines in a forehead that lay under his wheat blond hair; military style, crew cut. *Where are you now, I wonder?*

As his face dried, he let himself become absorbed into the land surrounding him. It was the reason he had come here in the first place, to get away from what had been his life, what could have been his life, to retreat and explore a long lost part of himself; the child he never really got to be. He was so busy being the man of the family it seemed the joyful innocence of his childhood had been snatched away. Now, as a grown man, when he felt so abandoned, so alone and so…homeless, it was the only place to which he could retreat, a place where it was safe and comfortable and warm; the dry, hot sun of the desert. He let his eyes simply wander over the side of the road at the field of saguaro cactus standing at attention like ghostly soldiers against the dusty gold and pink soil. It was the first time he had felt able to explore the freedom of his own soul, trapped for so long by the convention of his all-too-modern American life.

As he drove further out of the city, Joss replayed in his mind the moment of his decision, letting the calm of it soothe him like the old fad of Bio Feedback, or the new-agey Zen meditation. It was the big day, and he'd spent it all in court; the tense waiting, then having to air all of their dirty laundry in front of strangers. He was so humiliated, beyond anything he thought he could ever endure, like the judge shows he'd seen on TV, putting out all of their common business before an audience like trash theater. He was mortified.

When it was all said and done, he'd picked up a bottle of Patron and went to the rented room he had taken when he moved out of the house. He sat down with the bottle and his remote and hit the button. His thumb took him immediately to his favorite channel, *Encore Westerns; all westerns all the time.*

A noted mustachioed Western historian, resplendent with silver and turquoise bolo slide, belt buckle and rings was dressed in full period finery from his ten-gallon hat and duster coat to his gun belt and boots. As he strolled through the streets of a restored western ghost town, he offered snippets of history interwoven with legend almost as if he were inviting him, personally, him, Joss Meredith into *Tombstone* starring Kurt Russell and Val Kilmer.

At the sight of it, the bleeding thirty-nine-year-old heart of Joss Meredith ceased to exist, and the ten-year-old Joss took his place, sitting with one knee pulled up under his chin and his mouth hanging comically open giving real meaning to the old expression, *catching flies*. As the film's music came up, so did Joss's other arm, snapping off the light leaving only a colorful glow from the television reflected in the glassy gaze of the wide-eyed man-child. He pulled his leg in tighter, almost a ball of self-protection after all he'd been though during the day. He let himself go to that regressed state where he felt protected, the post-traumatic stress of the last few months slipping away in wave after wave of tequila, cowboy hats, boots, guns, and…*Arizona*.

By the time the end credits rolled, Joss knew what he was going to do. It had been decided in his mind without even having to translate itself into words. It was a good thing that he hadn't even begun to unpack his Army gear and make a permanent place for himself after his twenty-year retirement was official. It had been the smartest thing he'd ever done, joining the Army right out of high school. It was almost like there was never any other choice for him from the first time he sat down with the recruiter. The Army had trained him to be a solider, allowed him to get a college degree in Civil Engineering and after twenty years of service let him retire with full benefits, and all before he had officially turned thirty-nine.

And here he was, alone on the road to nowhere, with only the line of the slowly setting sun against the horizon in his rearview mirror to keep him company as he drove along that endless stretch of highway. He let it all replay itself in his mind as he stared aimlessly at the passing desert brush and rising mountain range, the radiant disc of light meandering with him on its journey downward toward the earth. The time seemed to pass so slowly, almost in slow motion as the sun continued on its path downward, increasing in its variation of colors; reds, oranges, ambers and yellows, casting shadows of the mountains, turning them into a vivid spectrum of dusky purples as he drove on.

He heard a beep, startling him out of the lulling hypnosis the dream-like climate, scenery, and colors had imposed on him, creeping quietly into the core of his being from the second he crossed the state line from California into Arizona. It was as if a switch had been flipped inside him, setting the clock of his future towards its uncertain end. Joss looked down at the sound at the gas gauge, and saw that it had dropped below an eighth of a tank, signaling the fact that he'd better keep an eye out for a gas station—the next one, in fact—since he had no real idea how frequently they might turn up on this stretch of road in this part of the country.

The sun had completed half of its lonesome cowboy ride through the sky when Joss saw the hazy light of some sort of civilization a little bit to the left of the off ramp labeled *Exit 164, Ak Chin Indian Community*. He breathed a sigh of relief and flipped on his right directional signal, heading to the right onto the ramp. As he pulled off the ramp at the other end, he looked up and saw a big red "K" above a covered set of gasoline pumps and a small Shop-Mart tucked behind the pumps. He coasted in and up to the pump.

While his tank was filling, he looked into the shop and saw a convenience store atmosphere, racks of merchandise, some commonplace and others, to his surprise, distinctly local. Inside he saw a hat rack that oddly reminded him of a singular ghostly soldier cactus he'd seen along the highway, except that this one had straw cowboy hats hanging from its arms. Joss smiled. *He couldn't, could he?* He looked around him. There were two trucks on both sides of him, all being serviced. He saw the men from the trucks. They were all wearing cowboy hats; one looked like an old prospector, another was clearly Mexican, short and dark with a black hat. A third was a Carhartt-and-broad-brimmed-brown-felt-hat man with a red bandana around his neck and skin as leathered as his belt and boots. Off to the side was a beat up, old faded blue pickup truck with the door open and a straw cowboy hat on the seat, but no driver. *Dammitall!* he thought to himself with a smile. He was no longer the majority out here, he was the minority. All the men seemed to have versions of these hats. He was the only man without one and it gave him his opening to take his childhood fantasy a step farther. The next thing he knew, he was walking through the door of the Shop-Mart and moving toward the hat rack as if it were a beacon to who he always wanted to be.

He stopped at the rack and self-consciously picked up a light-colored straw, roll up hat and put it on. He looked side to side and saw the pretty young brunette girl behind the checkout counter smiling at him. She shook her head and wrinkled her nose. He saw her point downward, indicating a hat on the bottom of the rack; still straw but darker and not as soft, firmer with a distinct brim. He picked it up and put it on, looking back to the counter girl who was by then smiling broadly and nodding, *Yes*, with a glint in her eye telling him that this hat had indeed hit the mark. She motioned with her hands to the sides of her head that he should take the sides of the hat and roll them up. He did as he was shown. The girl smiled again and nodded with satisfaction. Just then a figure stepped in front of her, blocking Joss's line of sight. It was a male figure wearing a blue and gold plaid flannel shirt with the sleeves cut off at the elbows, faded from wear, washing, and what appeared to be long hours in the sun. Below the shirt were old, worn faded jeans with a few natural (as opposed to self-made) tears. Below the jeans was a pair of dust laden, thick black leather, knee high muck boots with only a single strap across the arch of the foot and anchored with a silver buckle on the side, caked with drying mud.

The figure turned to see what the counter girl was craning her neck to see around him and Joss saw that it was a young man, slim but with the broadening shoulders of young adulthood, not tall but still growing, little more than a boy, seventeen or eighteen maybe. He had unintentionally messed short, dark blond hair above dark blue eyes, not brooding but lively, interested, bright and curious. His naturally pale skin was lightly spotted with blemishes and only beginning to show the dark blush of weathering from his increasing time in the sun, but was otherwise a well-scrubbed covering for his straight symmetrical features. He was not handsome in any particular way at this age, but in a few years that would change. In a few years, this boy could grow into his face and define what might be described as a *"real heartbreaker."*

The boy smiled an engagingly corn-fed smile at Joss, not perfectly straight teeth, but perfectly at home where they were nonetheless. The boy added a wink and a nod to it, then took his Big Gulp drink and stepped with a youthful bounce out through the door of the shop toward the old blue pickup truck that had been left with the door open. Joss paid for his hat and a cup of black coffee and headed out through the same door, a little bit more life in his step, too. He was feeling it. The hat gave him such a strange confidence, even more than his military uniform did.

Just as he got back to the black Jeep Wrangler he'd bought himself to celebrate his retirement from the Army, Joss saw the boy sitting in the blue pickup with the door still open. He had one booted leg dangling out over the seat and had put on his own straw hat, combining it with an oversized pair of mirrored aviator sunglasses; exactly the same kind Joss himself had buried somewhere in his gear cases from when he first went into the Army and Tom Cruise in *Top Gun* was the hot ticket. The boy tipped his hat at him and smiled that smile again, something so genuine about it, then slammed the door to his pickup and revved the engine, tearing off away from the station leaving a trail of dust behind him like a comet's tail streaming across the evening sky. Joss smiled with a small chuckle to himself, *Kids!* then, *Boys will be boys,* thinking that at that same age he was already on his way to being a full grown man. Then his smile changed, for all the very same reasons, reminding him of the wound that would hurt him until the day he died, laid open and hemorrhaging again. Overwhelmed by sadness and regret, Joss's normally broad, strong shoulders sagged, slumping down as he seemed to deflate. He wiped his eyes again and got back in his Jeep, slamming the door much too hard in his frustrated, blinding pain. He started up again and headed out, not having it in him to bother to leave a trail of dust like the boy had done.

He had just hit the ramp back onto I-10 when it overtook him; deep heaving, chest crushing sobs. "I hate you, you fucking bitch. I hate you. How could you?" he cried out loud to the interior of the jeep as his chest filled and emptied; heart-wrenching sighs of hurt and sadness. He had to pull himself together, take himself back to where he felt safe and comfortable. He looked back out of the window as the sun descended ever closer to the horizon, the colors so alive and vibrant, warming him from the inside as he headed closer to his dream, little by little, mile by mile.

By the time he reached the Gila Indian Reservation not long afterward, he had regained control of himself, searching in the dimming light for the small circles of trailers and shacks, signs of life that dotted the otherwise barren looking landscape along the highway for miles as he went. The colors of the sky took on a blazing, fire-like appearance as the setting sun came yet closer to the land below the mountains. Joss reached up and pushed the CD into the player, it was time for some company, even if it was only via music. He'd had it all planned. The slow, lonely guitar picking and strumming came through the speakers and filled the inside, then Don Henley's smooth, mournful, lamenting voice. *There's talk on the street; it sounds so familiar. Great expectations, everybody's watching you. People you meet, they all seem to know you. Even your old friends treat you like you're something new...Johnny come lately, the new kid in town. Everybody loves you, so don't let them down:*

the Eagles from when he was a kid, to help complete the picture, enhance the fantasy.

He had just started to sing along, watching as the sun hung low in the sky when he saw movement through the passenger-side window, a flash in his peripheral vision. He looked full to the right side and saw it running alongside him, a wolf or a coyote. It scared him to see that it was looking at him back and forth as it ran, like it was consciously trying to keep up with him. But that was impossible. He was going almost sixty miles an hour. *No animal could keep pace with that, or not for very long, not even a wild coyote, and why would it want to?* He felt the steering wheel jerk and the wheels swerve with it reminding him that he needed to pay attention to the road and less to the wildlife, but he couldn't help it. It was just so, eerie, so *unreal?* He looked back over to the desert alongside the highway. It was gone. Maybe it just got tired of spooking him. When he looked back up, he heard a growling rumble, mechanical, metallic grinding, an engine…and a big one, too. He looked in the rearview mirror and his heart dropped, a massive tractor trailer was on his tail, breathing down his neck. He could smell the exhaust as he hit the gas and felt the jeep pull away. In the next second he was deafened. The truck had blasted its whistle, shrilly igniting him into a primal, heart racing panic. Off to the side he saw the wolf or coyote was back, foaming at the mouth, running neck and neck with his front bumper. He felt a hard tap on his back bumper, seeming to push him forward while at the same time the animal darted across in front of him. He closed his eyes and jammed his foot down on the brakes, turning the wheel to get off the road before kissing his ass good-bye. The jeep skidded off to the side of the road on the right, jolting wildly as it hit the rough, rocky terrain over into a ditch alongside the road then stopped with a crashing thud. Joss's head lurched forward violently, slamming against the steering wheel then snapping back and forth like a bobble-headed crash test dummy, finally coming to rest in a slump over the steering wheel.

When he woke up, his head was throbbing to the sound of his own internal jackhammer. He felt his forehead and the huge swollen lump already rising there. When he brought his hand back down, he saw that his fingers were bloody. His eyes swirled in his head. *Where am I? What happened?* He reached for the door and pulled the handle. The door swung open and he set one foot on the ground. His eyes went gray and he tumbled out of the jeep, landing hard in a heap in the dust, then blackness. He was out again.

The next thing he knew he was on his back on the ground staring up at the blood red sky and the smattering of brooding clouds floating over him. Could he move? He didn't know. *You have to try.* He managed to raise himself up on his hands. His feet felt sturdier this time. He lifted himself up to standing and stepped back from the jeep. An old electric or telegraph pole was embedded like a log splitter through the front end of the jeep. He'd had a crash. He remembered slamming on his brakes to avoid hitting an animal and being pushed off the road by the truck. *How much time had passed?* He looked to the sky behind the wreck and saw that the sun had still not completely set, but was little more than a sliver of light; a searing red so intense it made him squint his eyes. His internal CD player went off in his head, a twangy, western campfire guitar strum and Glen Frey's easy, soothing, good ol' boy's voice. *It's another tequila sunrise, stirrin' slowly across the sky, said goodbye. He was just a hired hand, workin' on the dreams he planned to try, the days go by.* He reached up to his shirt pocket for his phone then remembered that it was now destined to be an artifact found in the desert by future generations. *Damn!* He made his way slowly back to the highway, although by then the shaking the crash had given him was starting to settle into his bones and muscles, his right leg giving way to a slight limp as he struggled to climb the small incline from the ditch to the road surface.

Back on the road, he looked around, surveying the area for what he could possibly do next. His eyes immediately seized on the orange neon light with a blue and white arrow

beckoning from about a half a mile ahead, and the small
building set back behind it off to the left. He couldn't quite
see what the sign read. His eyes were blurry, unfocused, but
whatever it was, it was a sign of life in the middle of the
desert. It was the only game in town, and his saving grace.

Keeping his eyes on the orange light, he put one foot in
front of the other awkwardly forcing himself forward to
whatever that sign offered. As he got closer, he could see that
the sign read *Reb's Diner*. From there he could also see the
bright lights shining from behind the plate glass windows
fronting the building that was apparently inside of *Reb's Diner*.
He saw the white neon light glaring from the center window,
*Open,* and he did what he had to do. He went towards the
light.

It could have only been minutes, but it seemed like hours
before he could put his hand up on the knob of the door and
turn it. He heard the tinny ring of an overhead bell, calling
Reb or whoever might be standing in for Reb to come to the
1950s style countertop surrounded by low, round, red-leather
covered chrome stools. With each step further inside, Joss's
vision widened and he could see that the countertop was not
the only part of Reb's that seemed to have been plucked out
of the 1950s or, more accurately, left relatively untouched
since then. A few seconds later, he heard a sound emanating
from an area behind the "Order Pick Up" window, then the
squeak of a set of red saloon doors separating the kitchen
from the dining area. He looked up to see a tall, full-figured
blonde woman, middle aged with teased, cotton candy hair
wearing dime store dangly earrings and make-up ten years
younger than she should have had; a man's brown plaid
cowboy shirt tucked into high-waisted jeans and a silver-and-
turquoise western buckle fronting her leather belt. When she
saw the red patch of half dried, half trickling blood on the
side of Joss's head, the blonde rushed around the countertop
and took him by the arm.

"You alright, Mister?" she squawked in a high pitched,
panicky voice tinged with a Southwestern sway. Joss gave a

bit of a weak nod and let himself be led to one of the round stools, sliding down onto it as soon as he felt it was safe to land. His ass had no sooner hit the seat when he put his arms down on the counter and laid his head on them. The blonde rushed into the back of the kitchen and came back a minute later with small white box with a big red cross on it in one hand and a warm damp cloth in the other. She put the box down on the counter and flipped the lid open.

"Come on now, Mister. Lift yer head up and let ol' Patsy take a lookatcha," the blonde said, identifying herself and putting her hand gently on Joss's shoulder.

Joss lifted his head slightly, turning it so Patsy could see the source of the blood. He closed his eyes as he felt the warm damp cloth touch his wound. He allowed himself to become absorbed by the gentle touch the woman had, telling him that this was probably not the first time she'd done something like this in her life. He felt her take his hand and lift it. She put the damp cloth in his hand and replaced it on his head.

"You just hold this here, Mister, and I'll be right back." She was back a few seconds later with a steaming hot cup of black coffee in her hand. She sat it down in front of him then reached under the counter by the cash register. When she pulled her hand back, there was a pint bottle of Jack Daniel's in it. She unscrewed the lid and poured in a shot's worth, then replaced the bottle into its home. "Take a sip of this, Mister. It'll help you get yer head right."

Joss picked up the cup and took a long swallow. The hot sting of the coffee combined with the hot sting of the whiskey coursed through his head like an electric current and he managed to straighten himself up. The blonde named Patsy had been right and he knew it was definitely not the first time she'd been through something like this.

"Care to tell me who beat-cha up?" Patsy said, lifting his hand from his head to look under the cloth and check on the wound. Satisfied that the bleeding was coming under control, she replaced his hand and the rag. "Should I be calling the police or somethin'?" she asked refilling his cup.

Joss spoke for the first time, a throaty Neanderthal style growl. "Car wreck. Ran off the road a little way back." He'd just finished his words when they both heard the rumbling sound of an old truck engine pulling up outside. It was only a matter of seconds before they heard the squeak of the hinge on the door and the sound of the bell from overhead and looked toward the sounds. It was the boy, the one with the shit-kicking boots and the pickup truck that Joss had seen at the Big "K" gas stop. Showing a decent upbringing, the boy removed his straw hat and aviator sunglasses before sitting down on a round stool over closest to the door and farthest from Joss and Patsy.

"What'll it be, son?" the big blonde brayed across the room.

"Just a coffee, please, Ma'am," the young man called back politely. His voice was deep, maybe even intentionally so, and very masculine in its tenor and the way he formed his words.

Patsy made her way over to the other side of the counter with a cup in her left hand and a coffee pot in her right. She set the cup down before the boy. Filling the cup with one hand, she pushed the creamer and sugar toward the boy with the other; a real waitress of the old school.

"No thank you, Ma'am, I take mine straight up," the boy replied to her silent gesture, but never taking his eyes off of Joss with his head still down at the far end of the counter. The boy saw Joss's distress and the now blood-tinged cloth in his hand.

"Is there something I can do to help, Ma'am?" the boy asked genuinely and pointed to Joss. Patsy motioned with her hand as if she were holding a cell phone and leaned into the boy to whisper.

"He says he crashed down the road. We need to report it and get somebody down here." The boy nodded that he understood, got up from his stool and reached into his pocket. He excused himself politely to the woman and walked toward the door marked "Restroom."

By the time the boy came out again, Joss was waiting to go in having regained both his composure and sure-footedness from the coffee tonic Patsy had made him drink. They looked at each other. What might have been a fleeting glance lingered much longer. The boy broke the gaze first, moving to walk past Joss, but side-bumping him in his haste. "Sorry, Sir," the boy said as he retook his stool, not looking back. Joss couldn't help but follow the boy's movements with his eyes, thinking, *What is with this kid?*

When he came back out, Joss passed behind the boy's back on his way to his own seat, but something had changed. The boy was no longer on the farthest end of the counter from him. He had moved three or four seats closer to where Joss was sitting. Joss looked over. The boy was staring at him. The look in his eyes was bold and confident on the surface but shy and afraid underneath. The boy looked away quickly and sipped his coffee.

"Can I get ya something else, son?" Patsy asked the boy.

"No, Ma'am. I got just enough money fer this coffee and one play on that jukebox of yers over there." With that the boy got up and went behind where Joss was sitting toward the neon-lit jukebox. As he passed, the boy walked so close to Joss again that he briefly brushed against his back.

*Are you doing this on purpose, kid?* Joss thought, but said nothing. He heard the sound of the metal coin clank through the slot into the music box, then the clicking sound of the boy's fingers as he pressed the buttons. The old-fashioned record dropped down and the music began to play; a weary, world worn piano. The blood in Joss's heart began to surge through his chest in a wave making it thump wildly. He fumbled for the napkin close to his hand and wiped the wetness from his face, then Glen Frey's voice again, this time trail dusty and cautionary: *Desperado, why don't you come to your senses? You been out ridin' fences for so long now. Oh, you're a hard one know that you got your reasons. These things that are pleasin' you can hurt you somehow,* came from the neon-lit box, stabbing Joss in the heart right where he lived, releasing another gush from his soul.

The boy came back and sat down, this time another three or four stools closer to Joss. Joss looked up. He saw the boy eyeing up a big cherry pie under a clear glass cover. Patsy saw it too.

"Ya sure you don't want a piece of pie, son?" The boy stood up and reached into both his pockets, coming back out with a single dollar bill and some small change in one hand and a few large bits of change from the other.

"I ain't got it, Ma'am. And I don't get paid 'til tomorrow night," the boy said and sat back down to sip his coffee. Joss and Pasty's eyes met, unspoken words passing between the two adults.

Joss looked over and saw the boy's hands, hard worked and so dirty; auto grease, dust, dried mud. Joss spoke before he knew what he was going to say. It just seemed to come so naturally to him.

"Go get washed up, and scrub those hands good. Tell the lady what you want for dinner," Joss's deep, even voice rang out in the silent echo of the room. The boy's face lit up brightly.

"Really, Sir?" the boy asked with a bit of an excited squeak, sounding his age for the first time. Joss just nodded and turned to Patsy.

"He can have whatever he wants. It's on me." Patsy smiled knowingly and nodded her approval. The boy jumped up, ambling toward the restroom like a new-born colt's first time through the barn door.

"Anything Tex-Mex, Ma'am. Burritos, tacos, enchiladas, rice, beans; nice and spicy and hot," trailed on the air as the restroom door closed behind him.

With that, Patsy took the damp cloth from Joss's hand and wiped the wound clean, gently. Once cleaned, she brought out a butterfly Band-Aid from the white box, pulled his wound closed and taped it shut. Just as she was finishing,

Joss heard the sound of heavy booted feet shuffle next to him. When he opened his eyes again, the boy was standing in front of him with his right hand out, his dark blue eyes glowing with sentiment; the expression on his face so serene, contented. Joss took his hand and shook it. The boy spoke.

"I'm Ben, Sir."

"I'm Joss, Joss Meredith. Nice to meet you, Ben," Joss said and let the boy's hand go. The boy sat down next to him then, and even closer than that, seeming to lean into him, shoulder to shoulder.

Patsy was out a minute later with a small bowl of leafy green lettuce crowned with a wedged tomato and sliced red onion. "Let's getcha started with this to keep ya busy while I'm out back cookin'," she finished, swinging around with a with a chrome wire dressing bottle holder and setting it before the boy.

"Much obliged, Ma'am," Ben smiled and pulled the bowl of salad close to him, picking up his fork along the way. Joss felt a playful nudge to his elbow from the side. "Thank you, Sir. That's real kind of ya," the boy said softly as he leaned into him again. "I really appreciate this." Joss nudged his own elbow back, playful in kind.

"Eh, don't mention it, kid. A growing boy needs to eat," Joss grumbled, taking the folded, red and white checked napkin from next to Ben's hand and shaking it out, handing it to the boy and pointing to his lap. Ben got the hint and did as he was instructed, placing the napkin neatly across his lap. The throbbing in Joss's head was not only *not* getting better, it was getting worse. He pulled his body away, shying away from the boy who seemed to lean even closer into him. The boy wanted his attention and would have it.

"I saw from your truck that you're a military man. All those stickers ya got all over yer windows and bumpers are so cool. I really admire that, Sir. Respect whatcha done fer yer country," the man-like voice came from the boy to Joss's side. Joss turned to look directly at the boy now. He had to. He couldn't resist. He was met by the boy's sincere gaze, not mocking or jesting like a smart ass kid might. Joss smiled weakly, the first one since he'd hit that pole.

"Really?" Joss asked incredulous.

"Yep," the boy affirmed with a solid adult-like nod, unequivocal. "Ya must be very brave," Ben finished then shoved a forkful of salad hungrily into his mouth, crunching a long leaf of lettuce bite by bite toying like a small kid might do slurping on a long string of pasta. "All those guns 'n bombs going off all 'round ya," Ben said and took another big mouthful, crunching loudly.

Joss sat up straighter and pulled his shoulders back like he used to when he was back at a base. He had to set a good example for this kid, just in case he decided on a military career of his own somewhere down the line, but more than that, he found out that inside himself he wanted to set that example.

"It's a hard life," Joss replied, "but it's been a good one for me. No regrets." The boy nodded thoughtfully with his mouth full again. Just then Patsy came through the red saloon doors doing her real old-time waitress thing again by balancing a few plates on her arm. She slung them down on the counter with a flourish in front of the hungry, "growing boy" staring at the plates: one plate with a big beef and chili burrito, a side plate of refried beans and rice and another smaller one with sour cream and picante bowls.

"Wow!" Ben let out, wide eyed with the possibility of his eyes being bigger than his stomach, but he was sure going to give it a try. A second later he had the fork back in one hand and a knife in the other, hacking at the burrito with youthful abandon. Patsy laughed out loud.

"Take it easy there, wrangler, it ain't goin' nowhere," she twanged. Ben smiled, first at Patsy, then at Joss.

"I feel like I could eat a horse, today, Ma'am."

"Okay, well then, just pace yerself," and she pointed at the cherry pie under glass, reminding him to save some room.

As the boy chattered with the waitress, Joss's head began to swim, a wave of nausea coming over him in a rush. He started to sway and slide off his stool. "Is someone coming to get me?" he asked, struggling to keep himself up and not lose his dignity in front of strangers. He grasped the edge of the countertop and held on. He heard the boy's voice quietly in his ear and felt his hand on his arm, pulling him back up on his stool and holding him there.

"Just take it easy now, Sir. Help is on the way. I made the call m'self. It shouldn't be long now, I promise. I'll set right here with ya." The two men looked at each other betraying an unspoken spark of trust that seemed to breach the twenty years, the lifetime that separated them.

"Go ahead and finish your dinner, kid," Joss rasped, embarrassed by the openness he saw in the boy's guileless eyes and at not being able to shield what lay bare beyond his own. He struggled to maintain his steely military presence but was finding it harder by the second as he sat next to this strange young man, like a character from a John Steinbeck novel, and feeling what? *sad? sick? afraid? weak?* He couldn't help but look into this boy's innocent face again with his clean scrubbed skin, blemishes and all, searching him with his eyes, forcing him to face his loneliness and grief like a mirror to his soul. His mind raced through it all so rapidly, ricocheting randomly like the little steel ball of an old-fashioned pinball machine off the little colored markers of who he really was, reading: *Fondness...Affection...Communion.* What was happening to him? *Desperado, oh, you ain't gettin' no younger. Your pain and your hunger, they're drivin' you home. And freedom, oh freedom well, that's just some people talkin'. Your prison is walking through this world all alone.*

Patsy was back just a few seconds later with an ice pack. "Let's try this," she said and held the ice pack to the injured part of Joss's head. He felt chilled a little but let her have her way. He steadied himself and took the ice pack from her hand and held it to his head. It did help. His eyes cleared and his thoughts seemed less murky, like a fog was beginning to lift. He glanced to the side to see Ben shoveling bite after bite of burrito into his mouth, followed by mouthfuls of beans and rice. The way the boy ate was almost mechanical in its efficiency, punctuated by a couple of good long chews and a few groans and sighs of satisfaction. "Ummm, ummm!"

Joss found that just the act of watching him eat so heartily and enjoying it so much made him feel less empty inside himself. It was almost like the delight one gets from growing things, well-loved plants, feeding them, nurturing them, watching them grow day by day, the right amount of sunlight and water, and when done just right, the wonderful product of nature it created.

"Whew! That wuz sure good," Ben said with a sigh, sitting back with his arms up and folded behind his head. Patsy sashayed over, none too graceful considering her size, and swooped up the empty plates. She looked at the boy with his arms so wide behind his head and saw a pendant that hiked up around his neck peeking out of the top of his white V-neck tee shirt. The symmetry of it spoke to her subconscious and made her smile. The pendant was silver and of Native American design; an eagle with its wings spread and its head turned to the side. The way the wings were spread reminded her of the way the boy's arms were spread out behind him, elbows out to the side. The silver was inlaid with light blue turquoise which stood out making the color of the boy's eyes less dark and there was coral inlay around the eagles head contrasting against his skin.

"My, that's a beautiful necklace, son. Did you get that around here?" Patsy asked, moving in to look just a little bit closer. The color came up in the boy's bashful face. He shrugged and turned sheepishly away.

"I don't rightly remember, Ma'am. It just seems that I've always had it, I think, but thank ya," Ben said as if he were searching his memory for a better answer and frustrated that he couldn't come up with anything better for the nice lady who'd just fed him. Patsy leaned over the counter to get a closer look.

"Well, it sure is pretty, and it suits you well," she said, now squinting to see the detail better, then she was back taking the dishes to the kitchen. The two men heard her call back out, "So, do ya think yer ready for a nice big piece of that pie?"

Ben brightened up again, his eyes taking on a mischievous glow and his smile a devilish grin. "I sure bet a big ol' scoop of vanilla ice cream would go real good with that pie, after all I am…a growing boy," Ben smiled, trying his best to be disarming without even know that there was a word for it, but knowing enough to cleverly use Joss's own words to punctuate his point and drive it home; straight into Joss Meredith's bleeding heart. He turned to Joss with another playful nudge of his elbow to get his attention again.

*Why are you doing this, kid?* Joss thought but caved in like a rickety old roof from any of the old abandoned silver mines surrounding them in the landscape. "Give 'im two if he wants," Joss said with a small self-conscious smile and an approving nod to the waitress. Something in the boy's eyes changed then, a wisp of sadness, longing. He put his hands up and unhooked the chain around his neck, holding the pendant dangling. He reached over and put it in Joss's hand just as Patsy was coming back through the red saloon doors.

"Wha?" Joss managed to get out, looking up at the boy, into his changed eyes, feeling dazed and not understanding.

"You don't have to do this, kid. It's only a dinner and I got a job, a real one, too. It's okay," Joss grumbled and tried to push it back.

"Please, Sir, for your kindness," Ben said with an insisting firm squeeze of his hand, his eyes suddenly taking on the sheen of wetness.

Joss looked bewilderedly up at Patsy standing in front of him, her hands on her big curvy hips, nodding to him that he should take it. Seeing the need for feminine intervention between the two masculine entities, Patsy reached in and took the chain from their hands and held it out end to end before her, then reached in close to Joss and put it around his neck, shifting her own body around him to hook it.

"Now, there!" she said with a *ta-dah* flourish, proud of herself for doing what she somehow knew needed to be done. Joss felt humbled, embarrassed by his own inability to communicate what he was feeling. It was all so new to him, but at the same time somehow strangely familiar. *Déjà vu?*

"Okay, give the boy his pie and ice cream…and chocolate sauce, too, if he wants. He's still got lots of growin' to do," he said gruffly with a sigh of mildly stagey exasperation as his male ego defense mechanism dictated.

"Yee-Haaa!" Ben shouted with enthusiastic bravado.

Again Joss watched as the boy devoured the huge plate of ice cream with chocolate sauce over pie, and again felt the empty well inside himself begin to fill up. This time he allowed himself to drink it all in, bite after bite, like the glug, glug, glug of a thirsty gas tank. As he watched he felt the drumming thumps that had littered his brain begin to ebb, fading into the distance like one of those dusky purple mountain ranges in his rearview mirror as he drove closer and closer to his dreams, receding away into some far nether region where they would trouble him no further.

Suddenly his hand felt disembodied, moving like it had a life and a mind of its own, up and toward his neck. He felt his fingertips lightly touch the silver and turquoise eagle they found there. It comforted him, eased his pain and made him feel somehow, whole. It was as if, in that flash of a second, the single piece of the puzzle of his life, long sought but always missing had been placed snugly into its perfect fitting space. When he looked up again, the boy, Ben, was staring at him, dark blue eyes so full of emotion wanting to say so much, trying to say so much. He put his fork down on the plate, reached up and touched the silver eagle around Joss's neck, then got up and went over to the jukebox again. Joss heard the clank of the coin and the tap of his fingers again. *It's another tequila sunrise, starin' slowly 'cross the sky, said goodbye. He was just a hired hand workin' on the dreams he planned to try, the days go by.*

A moment later the boy was back at the counter, on the stool next to him. He moved his hand over to Joss's, taking Joss's hand in his own, fingers entwined, clasped tightly. Joss didn't know what to do. It all seemed so natural to him. He looked down towards the clasped hands and gasped. What he saw made his eyes fill. Long streams of water began to trickle down his cheeks. The hands were almost identical, like each hand was part of a pair, shared by the same person. One was a little bigger, a little older, but they were the same. Joss looked back up at the boy, wiping his face with the other hand. The boy spoke quietly, calmly and respectfully, long streams of water flowing from his own eyes and down his face.

"It's time to go now," Ben said quietly, almost a whisper.

Joss nodded and stood with him, neither letting go of the other. Joss reached into his pants pocket with his free hand and pulled out a fold of bills, tossing it carelessly on the counter. As he did, a folded yellow sheet of paper fell to the floor, landing next to the stool where he'd been sitting. They walked slowly to the door with the bell, and went through.

From the back, Patsy heard the bell and hurried to dry her wet, soapy hands. Joss and Ben walked into the parking lot, seeming to glide toward the beat up, old blue pickup truck. Out of the corner of his eye, Joss saw what looked like multi-colored brightness of light in the distance, not far from where he'd left his car; fire, red flashing lights. Joss's heart started to pound, like a stalked animal, wildly in his chest, mortal fear. *I don't understand. I'm afraid, so afraid!*

"Don't look at it, Dad," Ben said, gently, lovingly, squeezing Joss's hand tightly. "You don't have to be afraid. We're together now. Just hold my hand tight and look at me."

Back inside Reb's Diner, the big blonde waitress named Patsy came pushing through the red saloon doors into the dining room. She didn't think she had to worry about those two. They didn't seem to be the type to stiff her for a meal. She came around the counter to where the man had sat, her eyes scanning around her, first the countertop, and saw the bills on the counter; a few tens and fives, much more than what he owed her. She looked down at her feet and saw the folded yellow piece of paper next to the stool. *It must have fallen out of his pocket when he left the money.* She bent over in a ladylike half kneel and picked it up. As she did, she glanced up through the plate glass windows at the front of Reb's and saw the two figures holding hands and walking into the darkness of the parking lot. *Huh?*

Her first reaction was to go after them. That paper could be something important. She rushed over to the door and threw it open, waving the folded yellow paper in her other hand. "Hey! Mister, you dropped…" but before she could finish, she saw that they were gone. The parking lot was empty. All she could see were the last remnants of a small fire down the road and a few cherry topped police cars next to it. She walked slowly back into the diner, holding the yellow paper and wondering, *Could it be important enough to mail it to him, maybe there's something in it to tell her who he was and where to send it.* She stopped in the middle of the floor under the bright light of Reb's Diner and unfolded the yellow paper. The heading at the top of the receipt-like paper read:

**Glen Arden Women's Health Center**
**2011 Santa Rosita Blvd.**
**Los Anos Perdidos, CA 90553**

Patsy read down the piece of paper to the center of the sheet.

**Patient: Jannelle Meredith**
**Service Provided: Pregnancy Termination**

**The End**

# ONE LITTLE INDIAN BOY

*"Indian tom toms are a drummin', desert winds are a humming…
humming an Indian lullaby…his hair is black, his eyes like a raven, he
sits in the saddle like his dad and when he grows up he's gonna be a
brave 'un and make his mommy glad."*

One Little Indian Boy,
Gene Autry (1949)

G eneva Sutherland picked up the tin-covered medical chart from the slot outside of the sterile looking hospital room and flipped the lid open. She scanned the chart rapidly as she'd learned to do early in her thirty-year nursing career. Her lips moved unconsciously as her eyes shifted further down the page, "Mack Guthrie, age 44." She read further into the diagnosis and treatments schedule. *Pneumonia,* she thought, shaking her head as she turned the corner into the white room containing two beds, each separately cocooned in pale blue curtains. A middle-aged, business-suited man was shifting uncomfortably in a chair in front of the half opened curtain farthest from the door. Her patient had a visitor.

"How is our patient this evening?" Geneva's island-lilted voice came around as she approached the bed. Her acute sense of people told her the suited man was as jumpy as a long-tailed cat in a room full of rocking chairs. He was holding a magazine in his hand, rolled up and anxiety worn. The man stood nervously, tossing the magazine down on the patient's tray table before launching into a twitching pace in front of the bed.

Geneva frowned at the man for failing to respond to her question out of courtesy. She looked down at the magazine: a copy of *Time*. The cover photograph was of a man in his mid-forties in front of a patchwork backdrop papered with poster-sized, blown-up pictures; iconic male figures of American literature from Hemingway to Hammett mixed amid the book covers of Jack London's *Call of the Wild*, James Jones' *From Here to Eternity* and James Dickey's *Deliverance*. The pictured man was good looking in an intellectual sort of way: a youthful mop of light, sandy brown curls crowning the emotionally honest features of a thinker. Wide and firm, his nose, forehead, cheekbones and lips gave away his northern European, possibly Nordic, ancestry. His eyes were a piercingly intense pale green sparkling with a mirthful intelligence and shielded from the world by small, round, gold-framed vintage eyeglasses giving him both an artistic and a wizened look. His smile was slightly turned up at the ends giving the impression that he was the only man in the world who held one particular secret, one that he was hesitant to share with an undeserving world. He was holding a copy of a hard cover book in his hands. The caption read:

*A "Norman Mailer" for the new century?*
*Literary Bad Boy Mack Guthrie's blistering*
*Pulitzer Prize winning novel, God's Prisoner,*
*takes no prisoners.*

*Hrruummpppf,* Geneva thought to herself, none of that high toned stuff for her. If it wasn't a *Real Housewives of...some damn where* she couldn't be bothered. She shifted her gaze to her patient and began straightening his bedding. Her eyes finally glanced up to his face and her breath caught in her throat. Her eyes shifted back down to the magazine on the tray table, then back to the man in the bed, then back to the magazine. The name on the chart and on the magazine finally clicked in her head, *Mack Guthrie.* She stepped back with her hands on her hips and took another look. She had *Time*

*Magazine's* cover man, Mack Guthrie, in her hospital bed. A rough, sharp voice startled her out of her astonishment.

"Well? Is he alright?" the suited man groused from behind her, hovering so closely that she could feel his breath on the back of her neck. Just then the man in the bed opened his eyes.

"Yeah, I'm alright," a croaking, dry voice came from the body in the bed.

Geneva jumped where she stood—almost wetting herself. "Is there something I can get for you, Mr. Guthrie?" the nurse rebounded, her accent pronouncing his name as *Gut-Tree.*

"Water, please," Mack replied in little more than a whisper.

Geneva reached over and took hold of the light blue plastic water pitcher from the table next to the bed and poured water into a small plastic cup. Before she could finish, she felt a brusque shove to her side, rude...pushy. The suited man had wedged himself between her and the bed.

"How ya feeling, Mack?" his agent, Ned Glassman, asked anxiously, the edge of his sharp voice easing now that he could see Mack's eyes open again after three days of waiting. His nerves were shredded by the possibility of the loss of not only his best friend, but his meal ticket for the last ten years.

Mack smiled weakly and nodded but inside felt like he had a ten ton elephant sitting on his chest making it almost impossible to breathe. Ned sighed, wiping his face with his handkerchief.

Geneva reached in between the men with the cup of water for her patient.

Ned snatched the cup from her hand and leaned closely towards Mack's head. "I'll do it," the agent snapped at the nurse.

Geneva took a step back with one hand on her hip and pointed a finger at the suited man with the other. "Now, I've had just about enough of that, Mister *Whoever you are.* I'm not your maid, I'm not your waitress, and I'm most certainly not your wife. I have one job here and that's to take care of this man," she huffed and puffed moving in closer to Ned's startled face with her finger. "Now, if you would pleeeaasssee just step back out of my way and let…me…do…my…job!" the nurse finished with a forceful step toward the agent.

Ned retreated.

She put her hand on Mack's forehead to feel for a temperature the old fashioned way.

The cool palm of her hand felt good. Mack looked up into her coal back eyes, still simmering with indignation, now betraying more than a little worry that she'd overstepped herself and put her job in danger if the twitchy agent complained. Once satisfied that Mack's forehead was an acceptable state of only warm, Geneva reached down and took his wrist, feeling for his pulse, once again in the old fashioned way. Mack liked that, too. It made him feel that he was indeed, in good, capable and comforting hands. Their eyes met again, her simmering temper now down to a low, rolling boil.

Mack smiled and winked at her whispering quietly, "Ice cream, please."

"Comin' right up, Mr. Guthrie," Geneva said kindly in that telltale sing-song accent that went with her warm island smile as she noted the vitals on the chart, then turned to go. "I'll make sure the doctor is notified that you're awake now and the positive change in your condition," she finished as she headed back towards the door. Ned made it a point to move out of Geneva's way as quickly as he could until the coast was clear, then rushed back to his friend's bedside again.

***

"Good morning, or should I more appropriately say, welcome back," the little Asian man in the white doctor's coat said as he walked over to Mack's bedside, not lifting his head from the tin-covered chart in his hand to look directly at his patient.

"Either will do just fine, Sam," Mack replied with a gruff husk still in his voice and an exaggeratedly 'child about to be scolded' expression on his face as he put another heaping plastic spoonful of Baskin Robbins butter pecan ice cream in his mouth. The doctor looked up from his chart, a dire expression in his smooth narrow eyes.

"Do you have any idea how close to dying you were, Mack?" Dr. Sam Chang said with obvious restraint. Sam had known Mack since they had been undergraduates at New York University, fraternity brothers and the only patient to whom Dr. Sam gave concierge service. Mack had been his big brother and been the one to smack the hell out of Sam's ass with a hard wooden paddle in the old basement of the frat house during initiation week.

Mack turned his head to the side, away from the doctor, "No lectures, please, Sam. I'm really not up to it," he pleaded, but the doctor wouldn't be moved.

"That lousy, rotten...*celebrity*...lifestyle you live almost killed you. You were so run down that the bug you picked up resisted all the traditional antibiotics? I had to bring out the big gun stuff and hold my breath. It was just that close, Mack," Sam admonished with a stiff, deep, determined voice holding up his hand with index finger and thumb a small one-eighth of an inch from touching. "That close, Mack. You have to stop this. If you get sick again—flu, pneumonia, whatever—with your weakened lungs and immune system, I don't think I'll be able to control it and you will die," Dr. Sam continued, never raising his voice above conversational tone, but nonetheless stressing his words with his voice to drive his point home to his patient.

"No more booze or drugs, prescription or not, no more smoking...of anything...and lay off the women for a little while, Mack. They'll be the death of you, and the bankruptcy, too. Three out of your four ex-wives are already out there in the waiting room, dividing up your money according to their time in. Are you following me here, Mack?" Sam Chang said, craning his neck to make sure he could look directly into Mack's eyes.

He knew Sam was right, for all of his professional success personally he was a nuclear winter. Mack nodded, shamed by the behaviors that had led him to that moment, searching back into his friends eyes for the first time.

"I feel like I'm on a runaway train, Sam. A carnival ride that won't stop spinning, and I can't get off."

The stern expression on Dr. Sam's face softened, the doctor in him receded and the frat boy came forward. *In the halls! In the halls! In the haaaaaalllllllsssss of Delta, Delta Sigma Rho, Yeah!* He saw everything he'd always admired about his big brother appear magically on Mack's face for the first time in years; a brief flicker of a second where Mack was once again the emotional powerhouse who wrote words that made people stop and think about their lives.

Mack went on. "It's like there's a fire in my head, Sam, a whirling forest fire, ready to erupt out of me like lava through the crust of a volcano leaving me...empty, and the only way I can fill myself up again is with...well, you know," Mack said, his voice now smoothing out from the ice cream, still deep and resonant, but not as scratchy or coarse. "I don't know what to do, Sam," he said shaking his head low and slow, his eyes downcast.

Sam couldn't help but smile at the florid and oh so literary way Mack could describe things. He took Mack's hand. Both hands went immediately into a three part formation, a comical combination of fingers, clenched and curled, flapping fingers with a wrist twist hand tug; the Delta Sig handshake.

"You gotta get out of here for a while, regain your strength and rebuild your immune system before something else can grab hold of you. Get out of New York for the rest of the winter. Go somewhere warm and dry. Start a new project maybe, something different. Two more days here and you can go," Sam said sternly and moved toward the door.

"But when I let you go, I want to hear about your plans for that long, warm vacation. Mild, dry temperatures for your lungs, clean air, a month, six weeks. You can afford it," Sam Chang said with a commanding finger, working to keep a hard line before passing into the hall.

***

Mack's ears recognized the soft squeak of that footstep coming up behind him. The hands accompanying those feet held a large brown, pink and white Styrofoam cup, *Baskin Robbins,* with a few magazines and newspapers tucked under one arm. "Who is it?" Mack called out in a stagey voice without turning away from windows of the hospital solarium.

"It's meeeeee, Mr. Guthrie," Geneva cooed from behind. "How are you feeling?"

"Oh, I'm much better, thanks, sweetheart," Mack replied using his melted butter voice. *Oh, it curled her toes whenever he called her sweetheart.*

"I'm so sorry, Mr. Guthrie, They've been short-handed over in pediatrics so they transferred me over there," Geneva said making soulful Elsie-the-cow eyes at him as she handed him the Styrofoam cup overflowing with peach ice cream, along with the paper goods from under her arm. "I thought you might like to keep up on things while you're here. Not much, just a *USA Today,* a *New York Times* Arts Section from the Sunday paper and a *National Geographic* I took from the doctors' lounge."

"Wow, thanks so much, sweetheart," Mack said again and heard her titter from off to the side as she went to take a blanket from the sofa next to him. He reached down into the side of his wheelchair. "They're releasing me today anyway."

Geneva turned back and put the blanket over his lap, tucking it in the sides around him.

He pulled his hand out with a book and held it out to her. "I want you to have this, Geneva. I signed it for you on the inside, but don't look until you leave, okay?"

Geneva took a step back with one hand up to her chest and the other holding the book out to see the cover and read to herself, *God's Prisoner.* Her eyes got misty.

Mack put his finger to his cheek and tapped. "You may kiss me now," he said affecting a phony regal air.

Geneva leaned in and kissed him lightly on the cheek. If her skin weren't so dark, one might have seen the crimson blush that came up in her cheeks. "Thank you so much, Mr. Guthrie. I will treasure this for my whole life," then she burst into tears and ran out through the solarium doors and down the hall clutching that book for dear life. When she reached the privacy of a stall in the ladies' room in the nurses' lounge, she opened the book to read the inscription. Ten one hundred dollar bills slipped out and fell to the floor.

"Oh Lord!" Geneva Sutherland let out in a sharp, loud squawk, easing herself down onto the toilet seat, her mouth agape at what had just happened before turning again to the inscription. *"To Geneva, for saving my life in the sweetest possible way. Ever, Your Mack."*

Back in the solarium, Mack spooned heaping mouthfuls of peach ice cream into his face and flipped through the Sunday *New York Times* Art Section. *Boring!* He took the *National Geographic Magazine* from the pile next to him and looked at the cover. The spark of a forest fire ignited in his head. The picture was a landscape of golden sand desert, dotted with shadowy cactus below a startlingly vibrant sunset of reds, oranges and yellows taking the form of a Native American sand painting. The caption read: *New Mexico, The Land of Enchantment celebrates 100 years of Statehood 1912-2012.* He opened to the page of the lead article. The photo blocking of various sized and colored images above the title grabbed Mack's imagination and shook it like dust from a dirty old rug, glistening particles and cobwebs flying everywhere. *From Geronimo to Billy the Kid. New Mexico: Building Block of the*

*American West.* The spark in Mack's mind fanned into a flame and he knew what he would do next. *I'll go to New Mexico and write…a play. Yes! Yes! A Broadway play…of two characters, dusty, renegade staging. Conversations between Pat Garrett and Billy the Kid—after they were dead. Brilliant! And call it what? The Ghost of Billy the Kid. That's it!*

Raging, screaming, hot, violent, masculine, burning like wildfire in his head, Mack Guthrie's heart beat like a native drum at the rawness of it, the elemental nature of the conflict; the dangerousness, law and outlaw, friends and enemies, sex, alcohol, guns, betrayal and anger…so much anger. *That's it! Fucking incredible! Thank you again, Geneva!*

"Just what the freaking doctor ordered," Mack Guthrie said aloud with a great heaving sigh. It was like a giant, existential weight had been lifted off of his shoulders. He followed it with another large mouthful of peach ice cream, oblivious to the beads of sweat having formed on his forehead and beginning to glide their way down the side of his face from the heat of his fever, both the internal and external kind.

\*\*\*

"Can I get you something to drink while we're waiting for take-off, Sir?" the young, red-headed flight attendant said to the man crumpled up in the corner seat, unidentifiable under the thick canvas shirt and canvas winter coat, his face and head hidden beneath a large black pair of slick Harley Davidson sun glasses and black-knit thug hat.

"A double brandy in a cup of black coffee please," a deep, gruff voice came out from beneath the bundle, then paused. Sam Chang's cautionary voice echoed in his head, *No booze…* "And…a large orange juice on the side, please," Mack Guthrie ordered from the curious flight attendant with a slightly weak smile.

"Yessir," the young man said politely with a squeak in his voice, bowing and walking backwards, then turning to rush off to fill the order. After all, it was his first time assigned to first class and he wanted to make a good impression. As he walked away he heard a loud ringtone coming from the vicinity of the bundled man, *"Twenty, twenty, twenty four hours ago, I wanna be sedated.* The Ramones. Mack reached into his inner pocket and pulled out an IPhone. He looked at the lighted screen dulled by the tint of his sun glasses and saw the incoming number. "Oh, alright!" he said aloud to himself and hit the button.

"Hello, Ned," he said exasperated. "No, I'm not at the apartment. I'm not even in New York. As a matter of fact, right now I'm in a seat on a plane about to take off from Newark." Suddenly, the hand with the phone pulled away quickly from his ear, the screech coming from it radiating for five feet in any direction. When it subsided, Mack brought the phone back to his ear. "Are you finished now? I'm following the doctors' orders and taking a nice, long, warm vacation."

Mack paused to listen. "Oh, I guess it can't hurt now. I'm going to New Mexico, to the border towns along the Mexico line." He had to pull the phone from his ear again and hold it out to the air. When the tirade stopped again, he brought the phone close. "Just cancel them. Tell them the truth. I'm recovering from a tough bout of pneumonia and I need to rest." Another loud shriek came from the phone. Mack lost his temper and shouted back, "Will you stop fucking shouting already, Jesus Christ almighty, Ned, you'd swear I was cutting off your fucking leg," Mack barked, then in the break from the lower volume nattering asked, "Do you want to hear the upshot now? Yeah, actually there is one. You can spend the rest of the winter and early spring shopping around for a producer and theater to house the play I'm writing... Yeah, I want Broadway, a big house, too. Get the buzz rolling with the media," he said with a cavalier, self-satisfied inflection in his voice.

"Yeah, no, it's not done yet, but it will be…Yeah, yeah. I'm calling it *The Ghost of Billy the Kid*, two characters, real star vehicles for two powerhouse leads. See who you can get interested, too. Brad Pitt, maybe?"

Just then the red-headed flight attendant brought over a tray with Mack's order. Mack loudly faked his own take off. "Hey, Ned, plane's taking off. I need to shut down the phone for a while. I'll call you when I get there and get settled," then closed with an answer to Ned's last question, Mack replied brusquely. "Fuck her. She was too busy showing her ass around Hollywood trying to get noticed to even bother to come see me in the hospital. Tell her I'm dead." He hit the off button and took a long sip of his brandied coffee. The attendant stood by waiting for any further requests.

"Ahhh," Mack said with a satisfied glow in his voice. "Perfect. Just what the doctor ordered." He smiled at the boy, leaving him with a standing order. "Keep 'em coming till I fall asleep, will ya, son?"

"Yessir," the boy twittered excitedly. It was his first time meeting a celebrity and such a macho, handsome one, too. The flight attendant almost swooned where he stood. And the passenger had called him *son*, too. *So hot,* the boy thought as he rushed away to report back to the others about his special passenger.

***

Four hours later Mack felt a gentle nudge at his shoulder, his eyes opened slightly. It was his red-headed flight attendant. "We're almost there, Mr. Guthrie. I brought you another coffee. This one is plain," the boy said smiling and set the cup down on the unfolded seat tray.

"Thanks, Red," Mack grumbled and coughed through his coat-covered mouth.

The boy smiled, nodding and backing away. "We'll be on the ground in less than half an hour."

Once the plane had landed, the boy was back standing at attention before the bundled man. Mack stood slowly, his joints and muscles rebelling against his attempt to have them move, still creaky and painful from his hospital stay and not moving during the whole flight. He stumbled. The boy leapt to grab his arm. "Steady now, Sir," the red-head said quietly.

"Thanks, son," Mack growled, shaking it off as he slowly came out of his row and reached for his single carry-on from the overhead. When Mack turned around again, the red-headed flight attendant was standing at attention waiting to walk him to the exit door. Mack noticed that the boy had a rolled up magazine in his hand. When they got to the exit door, the boy stopped and looked at Mack sheepishly, youthful bashfulness washing over him like a fresh coat of paint. He unrolled his magazine. It was a roughed up copy of the *God's Prisoner* issue of Time.

The boy held the magazine out in one hand with a black Sharpie maker pen in the other, his green lashy eyes taking on a wide, adoring puppy-like quality. "Mr. Guthrie, would you please do me the honor?" he asked shyly, breaking the very first rule of first class travel: bothering the celebrities for things like autographs, but he just couldn't help himself.

Mack was so flattered. The kid was still just a boy and couldn't have any real appreciation for Mack's adult style of writing. He took the magazine and asked, "What's your name, son?"

"Ethan, Sir," the boy squeaked. He got goose bumps every time this man called him "son." S*oooo hot!*

Mack smiled, and signed the cover. *"To Ethan, thanks for the comfort. Be a good boy, son. Mack,"* and handed it back. Ethan read the cover and his face turned beet red, well outshining the brightness of his hair. Mack put out his hand and took the boy's giving it a good, firm shake.

The boy just stared at him stupefied. "I will never wash this hand again, Mr. Guthrie," Ethan said as Mack moved in closer to him to pass through the narrow tunnel to the exit.

***

With his face and head hidden beneath the sunglasses and hat with his collar up, Mack Guthrie headed down the deplaning tunnel into the airport itself toward what that *National Geographic* magazine had called, *The Land of Enchantment.* "Enchant me if you can. I dare ya," he mumbled to himself as he walked unhurriedly through the corridors, still not having gotten the kinks out of his muscles.

As he ambled along, Mack began to notice the enlarged photographs lining the walls around him: an art exhibit displayed against the long tunneling walkways to the various exits. Entitled, *"A Rancher's Life,"* it was an exposition of weather-beaten, craggy faces furrowed with cracks and crevices like road maps, witnesses to the hardness of their lives, their eyes so full of toil and pain, suffering and worry, but still revealing the strength within themselves to forge the rugged paths they had chosen; drought, outlaws, disease, famine, pestilence. Mack examined those faces closely as he passed into the main lobby of the airport, looking into their eyes as if they were standing right in front of him. Men leaning on their rifles, one with a Bible under his arm, propped up against rickety, unpainted clapboard outbuildings, some with farm tools, dressed in overalls, flannel, original dirty Levis and field worn boots.

With each photograph he passed, Mack began to answer his own question. Yes, indeed, he was becoming enchanted by this golden, rough-and-ready land, and now he could add a new feeling to his wide vocabulary of human emotions: *fear!* He was…afraid. *Afraid of what?* Of what might lie ahead on this journey to…*where? I don't know. To knowing myself?*

*** 

He drove out of the rental car parking lot in the rented Jeep Grand Cherokee and headed south from Albuquerque; that knotted feeling continually growing in his guts with each highway sign he passed, almost as if they were heralding his arrival into...*Billy the Kid country? The land of Geronimo?*

The wordless vision in his head as he drove was one of being in outer space, like the schlock space films he grew up on. He was an astronaut, floating weightless outside of his ship. Suddenly the tether to his ship snaps and he floats off, no longer attached to anything, completely adrift in unexplored space, disconnected to anything he recognizes with no hope of rescue: no Ned, no Sam, no ex-wives, no career, no children, no parents, no one. He was all alone with nothing but black, empty space; floating...floating...further and further away.

He found himself overwhelmed by the expanse of it, the magnitude of his isolation. His heartbeat ripped through his chest and tears pooled in his eyes as the blood coursed unrestrained in his temples. A half an hour outside of the city, he began to truly understand the immenseness of his *new space*. But it was not one of blackness and cold. It was one of golden sand, a living desert, rippling with the jagged ridges of the hills against the horizon as they glistened entrancingly below a soul-warming sun.

He turned on the car radio. A DJ's voice came out of the speakers, deep and whisky gruff with a southwestern twang. *"In honor of what would have been the one hundred and fifth birthday of America's favorite singing cowboy, Mr. Gene Autry, WKBX and ol' Dusty here will be playing all Autry, all day, and I'm proud and pleased to start the show by reciting what every man my age knows and which every young wrangler should learn, Autry's Cowboy Code, created for his young radio listeners aspiring to be like him. And it goes like this, a cowboy must:*

*Never shoot first, hit a smaller man or take unfair advantage;*
*Never go back on his word or a trust confided in him;*

*Always tell the truth;*
*Be gentle with children, the elderly and animals;*
*Not advocate nor possess racially or religiously intolerant ideas;*
*Help people in distress;*
*Be a good worker;*
*Keep himself clean in thought, speech, action and personal habits;*
*Respect women, parents and his nation's laws;*
*Be a patriot.*

*Alright, now, wranglers, cowboys and those who are in their hearts and souls, let's start with his early hits, and remember folks, it's Cowboy music, not country, big difference.* Autry's twangy voice came yodeling through the speakers to an upbeat guitar strum. *He's in the jailhouse now. He's in the jailhouse now. I told him once or twice, quit playin' cards and shootin' dice. He's in the jailhouse now.*

The wetness around Mack's eyes grew, intensified with every word that came out of those speakers. It was like Gene Autry himself had grabbed him roughly by the collar and was delivering a flurry of manly bitch slaps back and forth to his face for everything he was and was not. *Wake up, boy, and be a man!*

Nothing had ever really meant anything to him, not really. It was always *his* career, *his* fame, *his* desires, *his* needs, *his*...vices, sex, booze, drugs. *You really set some example out there, smart man!* What had he really accomplished in his life? He couldn't really say that anyone had ever really loved him? *And here you are driving off into the sunset to die like some beat down old cowboy. Would anyone care? Nah, the papers would make a scandal of it, TMZ maybe, but in the end, a week later he'd be lost to oblivion.*

He saw a small building over on the right side of the road. He wiped his mouth with the back of his hand. He sure could use a drink or a coffee. He drove closer. An unlit, hand-painted sign read: *Ro Bodean's.* Mack parked on the side of the old unpainted wooden building. It had the look of a small trading post right down to the cigar store Indian next to the door to greet the patrons; all wooden, with a porch held up by wooden columns. Indian horse blankets were thrown over the porch rails to dry and there was an old wooden screen door with a dingy paper sign hanging out front, "Open."

*This can't be real,* he thought and pulled out his laptop going straight to Google. His fingers typed G-E-N-E-A-U-T-R-Y into the search box and hit the go button. The screen exploded with entries; a man dressed to the hilt in his best cowboy duds astride his world famous horse, Champion, waving and smiling. A child-like "Wow" resounded in the truck as his fingers tapped away furiously.

Stoked by his new found...*what? Idol?* Mack got out and walked around to the front of the building. The screen door flapped slightly in the breeze. He saw a wooden counter that may have been a bar at one time; six tall wooden bar chairs, five of them occupied, old fashioned fly paper strips hanging from the ceiling with a big, planked, overhead fan making them sway. A particularly rusty hinge squeaked loudly announcing his arrival as he opened the door. He walked in slowly.

Whatever movement there was in the room stopped. Six faces, five on stools and a single woman's figure behind the bar were all staring at him. The men at the counter were all dressed similarly, faded Carhartts and jeans, and they all had hats, cowboy hats. It was so Clint Eastwood spaghetti western that it almost made Mack laugh out loud, but he didn't dare. He knew from the looks on their faces that they wouldn't laugh with him. It didn't dawn on him until he saw his own reflection in a dirty window next to him what he'd done wrong. He was dressed like some kind of over-aged, thug wanna-be. The knit cap and sun glasses didn't belong in the picture he'd just walked into. A few seconds and the men turned their attention back to the counter and their meals.

The woman spoke. "Not from around here are ya, Mister?" the tall, auburn-haired woman asked in a husky smoker's voice, one hand holding a dishrag on her hip and the other hand waving him in. "Have a seat, I'm Ro," the woman said with a sassy smile. She was about forty-five, well-kept and painted with thick black eyelashes wearing a tight fitting chamois cowgirl shirt with fringe around the yoke and down the front that showed off her still shapely figure, silver-and-turquoise earrings dangling down the sides of her face.

Mack sat down. The men at the counter all turned away from him, raising their shoulders against him exhibiting exactly where the old phrase, getting *the cold shoulder* came from. Mack held up his hands in bewilderment. Ro shrugged, mouthing to him through thick-painted red lips, and motioning with her hand. *The hat, the glasses, city slicker,* and she turned around with a coffee cup and pot in her hand. Mack reached up and removed his hat, stuffing it in his pocket as inconspicuously as possible then the sunglasses.

Ro leaned into him then, her husky voice almost vibrating in his ear. "You're real purdy, Mister," then leaned back again smiling mischievously to herself. "Looks like you could use a good meal though." Then she stopped and thought. She turned back to Mack, "You been sick, ain'tcha?" she said, more a statement than a question.

Mack nodded, keeping his eyes downcast.

Ro came back with a plate and set it down in front of him: two fluffy, flaky, golden country biscuits with a side of butter and strawberry jam. "Where ya headed, good lookin'?"

Mack looked up then, flashing his eyes at her in acknowledgment of her kindness to him. "I'm going down to Lincoln."

That got a few snide snickers from the men on the other stools.

"Let me guess, you're doing the Billy-the-Kid thing?" Ro asked with a sly smirk. He heard a riff of loud coughing from under one of the cowboy's hands on the other end of the counter, "Tourist!"

Ro turned and just waved her hand. "Don't pay them no never mind, Mister..." she said with the expectation of him finishing it and giving her his name.

He picked up her lead, "Mack, Mack Guthrie," he responded and put out his hand. Ro took it real lady-like and shook briefly. Mack nodded, flushing with embarrassment.

He broke apart a biscuit and put a piece in his mouth, moaning with satisfaction, "Ummmm, that's really good."

Ro smiled. "You bet it is," she said with a wink then turned with her coffee pot to the other men at the counter, refilling their cups like ducks in a row. When she came back to refill his cup she leaned into him again. "You need a hat, Mack, if yer gonna get along down here," she whispered as if telling him a secret.

Mack shrugged, unconvinced that he could ever pull off such a feat.

Ro turned again, this time displaying the rest of her shapely figure from behind. All the men turned to get a look. A second later she was gone into the back of the building. She returned a few minutes later with a big, dark clay-colored cowboy hat, clearly used over a long period of time.

"Here, take this," she said handing the hat to Mack over the counter.

His hand took it but his words said otherwise, protesting, "Oh, I couldn't. Thanks, I really appreciate it, but I can't. I'd feel so silly." The minute it came out of his mouth, Mack knew that was the wrong thing to say in front of all those men who clearly didn't feel the same way. Mack felt the bristling anger sparking from the other men from across the room like an electric current. Now he was obligated to take the hat and wear it, at least until he could get out of there.

"It was my husband's, but he ain't got no need fer it no more. Been passed near two years now," Ro said with a slight break in her voice and mist in her eyes. "It needs a good home. Please take it, Mister Guthrie," she said and wiped her eyes with her dishtowel.

Mack put the hat on, and it was indeed a perfect fit.

"Oh, my goodness," Ro exclaimed with decidedly girly inflections in her thick voice. "You look so handsome!" She put her hand to her chest, more mist. "Go look," she ordered and pointed to a rusted *Guess Your Weight* machine with a dulled mirror at the top.

Mack got up and looked. It was like he was seeing himself for the first time. He heard the DJ's voice from the radio show in his head. The cowboy code: *Never shoot first, hit a smaller man or take unfair advantage. Never go back on his word or a trust confided in him.*

Mack went back to his chair, not quite the same Mack that had been sitting there just a minute earlier. The first thing he noticed was that the other men at the counter no longer had their backs to him, no longer turned away from him. The cold shoulder seemed to have thawed.

One of them got up, a big ol' bubba with a beard and black outlaw hat. He dropped some money on the counter. "Thanks Ro," the buffalo-voiced bubba said then headed toward the door. He stopped behind Mack's back on his way. "Not so silly now, is it, Mister?" the bubba asked and slapped him ham-fisted hard on the back. Mack restrained the reflex to choke out loud, and found that he was kind of proud of himself for not letting on that the big ol' bubba had almost sent him flying across the counter.

"No, no, it's not," Mack said quietly to himself after the bubba had gone, finding himself humbled by the confession. Another man got up from the end of the counter; tall and sinewy, rangy and weary, in his sixties with skin like leather and a big graying mustache under a big gray hat. He reached over and put his money into Ro's hand.

"Thanks, darlin'. See ya next time." He stopped next to Mack and waited for him to look up. When Mack raised his head, he saw the same look in gray hat's watery blue eyes that Mack had seen in some of the pictures in the airport. The man spoke to him, a voice like an engine rumble. "Thar's a big storm a-brewin' down thar, comin' off the Gulf and headed fer Lincoln; could be real bad. Look after yerself down there, son, ya hear?" the old ranch hand said then shuffled off out through the door to his pickup.

Mack himself was up next, following their lead. It would be getting dark soon and he still had a long way to go. He reached into his pocket and pulled out a few bills, took a single hundred and held it between his fingers out to her. "Thanks, Ro," he said shyly... "for everything," and put the bill in her hand with a light, gentlemanly squeeze.

"You take good care of that hat, cowboy," she said misting over again then turned quickly to disappear behind the kitchen door. More Cowboy Code played in Mack's head as he walked back out through the screen door and got into his truck. *Respect women, parents and his nation's laws.*

He'd just gotten back on the road when Dusty the DJ was announcing another Autry song, *The Last Round-up.* Mack looked up at the sky and saw that the old rancher was right. Off in the distance a mass of brooding black clouds was gathering from the southeast toward the west. He was struck first by the beauty of the color palette it created in the sky; indigos, purples and blues that his mind couldn't have imagined, pushing its way in, eclipsing little by little the glowing colors of the sunset as the storm rolled further and further over the southern horizon. Autry's forlorn voice came crooning through the speakers. *"I'm headin' for the last round up, gonna saddle old Paint for the last time and ride. So long old pal. It's time your tears were dried. I'm headin' for the last round up. Git along little doggie, git along."*

It wasn't long before the first drops of rain hit the windshield as he drove headlong into the blackening sky. Only a few at first, then more and more with each mile until it seemed like one long sheet of water was washing over his windshield. Something primal in him sent up red flags. His nerves started to jangle and the hairs stood up on his arms as he clenched the wheel tightly, fending off the blankets of rain beating against the truck, the wind acting as if it were intentionally trying to push him off the road.

The sky got darker by the mile until he was engulfed in pitch black with only violent cracks of lightning hitting points in the desert, illuminating the surrounding landscape with the intensity of a rescue flare in the distance. DJ Dusty was announcing another song, a lively guitar strum and Gene Autry's distinctive voice rang out. *Indian tom toms are drummin', desert winds are a hummin'. Ten little, nine little, eight little Indians, seven little, six little, five little Indians, four little, three little, two little Indians, one little Indian boy.* Bolt after bolt of lightning ignited random patches of desert with bursts of strobe light, each landing closer and closer to the road, flashing glimpses of cactus, rock formations and patches of tall weeds.

*His eyes are black, his hair like a raven, he sits in the saddle like his dad. When he grows up he'll be a big brave 'un and make his mommy glad,* Gene Autry sang out into the storm. Another enormous clap of thunder exploded. *I have a hunch he's a good little Indian…* A jagged sliver of lightning ripped the night sky in two as it delivered a smoking strike to the ground close to the road as Mack passed. The Jeep trembled underneath him…*one little Indian boy.* Mack felt like he'd been physically yanked out of his own skin. Blinded by the intense flash, the speed of his heartbeat made his breathing rapid and labored. He held on to the steering wheel white-knuckled until the truck came to a rolling stop on the side of the road.

The Jeep was dead. The dashboard panel was black, no electricity. When his breathing returned to normal, he tried to get the engine to turn over all the while knowing what the result would be…no power. *Fried!* A cough rattled in his chest as he reached into his pocket for his IPhone to call roadside assistance. It was dead, no power, no light. *Gone.*

"What the hell do I do now?" he sighed aloud to the empty truck, the dampness having sent a chill up his spine. The rain beat down furiously on the roof, like he was being attacked by an army of monsters bent on his destruction, desert zombies in the pitch blackness of the desert night. And it seemed to be getting cold, or he was getting cold, or hot. He felt his forehead. It was warm. He was getting sick again. He could feel it, and he was stranded, miles from anywhere, in the dark, in the rain. *Think, Mack, think. It's what you do for a living. Don't panic and think it through.* He answered himself out loud. "Wait it out. It can't rain forever. And when it stops…get out and walk to the nearest town."

He closed his eyes and waited, nodding off not long after to the *tap tap tap* of the rain on the hood like a mystical spell with the gusts of wind rocking him in the Jeep like a baby in a cradle. When he awoke, it was an hour later and the rain was still coming down in buckets. The dampness had seeped further into him and the temperature seemed to have dropped even more. He felt his head again. It was more than warm, verging on hot. Sam Chang's dire voice replayed itself in his head. *"...if you get sick again...I don't think I'll be able to control it and you will die."*

Pressure started bearing down on his chest again. He struggled to suppress the coughs, pulling his coat up closer around his neck, trying to convince himself that nothing was happening. *You have only two choices and each of them will kill you. You can stay here and hope for someone to come by and if no one comes, die here of a chill Sam can't cure. Or, you can try to make it to the nearest house or town on foot and die of a pneumonia Sam can't cure. How do ya wanna die, smart guy?*

He answered himself. *Staying meant a slow death if no one came, but if he got out and walked he might come across a house or something close.* The rattling cough in his chest forced its way out with a vengeance bringing the reality of his situation home. *Die like a man, at least fighting for your life* was his last thought before he secured Ro's husband's hat firmly on his head and forced his aching body to get out of the truck. The wind blew him back at first. *Just keep your head down and keep moving,* he thought as he struggled to stay on the road surface with the rushes of water covering his feet.

He was soaked to the skin in minutes, still clutching the collar of his coat up around his neck. *How long can you do this?* Not long, he knew that. *Keep an eye out for a house or lights alongside the road,* he had to keep reminding himself. The stinging rain made it difficult to look anywhere but down. He'd gotten about two miles before he felt the chill again, running up his legs through the length of his back and up the nape of his neck, his muscles contracting into one huge spasm. He stumbled and almost fell. *Another mile,* he kept telling himself. *There's got to be something ahead soon*, but when he looked up all he saw was darkness.

Another mile and his pace had slowed to almost a crawl. The tightness in his chest grew with each step, squeezing the breath out of him, making it hurt to even cough. It got harder to pick up his feet. His breathing became little more than a heaving wheeze, and he was burning with fever now. His eyes swam with it. *I'm going to die here. I can't do this anymore.* His pace slowed down to single steps going…nowhere…in the dark. His head began to swirl and his vision narrowed.

*One more step, Mack. Just one more step.* He looked around one last time and saw a light; a tiny, dim orange glow in the dark distance of the desert off to the side of the road and the shadow of a small shack behind it. He took one step in that direction and fell to his knees, tumbling down the shallow incline into a water-filled ditch.

He looked up to find the light again, lifting himself on his hands and knees, forcing them to crawl towards it. His chest rattled thickly then blew up into a racking cough. His body shuddered once and he fell to the ground, his face half submerged in a muddy puddle of desert. *Good-Bye.*

***

A cool rag on his head was the first sensation he recognized, and a smell; herbal, menthol, earthy. He opened his eyes just slightly. His vision was weak, blurry, as though he was looking through thick gauze. He could see the small dark silhouette of a figure lit from behind by the warming glow of firelight against vividly patterned cabin-like walls.

His eyes strained to focus and Mack found himself being gazed upon curiously by a small boy, about nine years old, reddish-amber skin, coal black hair cut short and wide, almond-shaped, jet-black eyes with a very serious look in them. The boy's features were strong-boned but softened with leftover baby fat giving him a stocky appearance, and his ears, thick lobed and sticking slightly out, reminded Mack of the number eight divided down the middle with each side placed on a side of the boy's head: a Native American version of a Raphaelite angel come to life.

"Hello," the little reddish-gold boy said shyly.

"Hello…Who are you?" Mack rasped in a whisper.

"I'm Joseph…Broadfoot," the little boy said like he was reciting a poem. "Who are you?"

"I'm Mack…Guthrie…Where am I, Joseph?" Mack asked softly, still not sure he could lift his head.

"At the house of my grandfather," Joseph replied. "Grandfather calls you 'Big Voice'." The boy got up then and reached to a table next to the bed. He brought back a small wooden bowl. Holding it so delicately, he raised the bowl up close to Mack's face. "Grandfather says you must drink as much of this as you can," and he raised it close to Mack's lips, his eyes determined but fearful, looking at Mack the way a white child might look at the wild animals at a circus or zoo.

Mack took a sip expecting the worst, a homemade poison to make him gag. But he was wrong. It was sweet, like honey and berries, rich and thick, some sour and slightly bitter. "Ummm that's good," Mack said making a funny lip-smacking face. The little boy laughed, his black orb-like eyes now proudly glistening in the firelight at his accomplishment of getting the white man to take his medicine.

Mack found that he could raise his head a little and tried to push himself up on his elbows. Joseph was right there with a rough fabric-covered pillow for the back of Mack's head. "Where is your grandfather, Joseph?" Mack asked, curious as to how such a small boy would be left alone so long with a total stranger in this country, sick or not.

"He's hunting," Joseph said matter of factly.

"And he left you here alone?"

Joseph nodded, making his straight black hair sparkle in the firelight. "To take care of you," he said like a dutiful little man.

"Well, that's an awful lot of responsibility for a little boy. Don't you think?" Mack said, beginning to enjoy this unusual interaction.

"I'm going to be a big chief someday," the little raven haired boy called Joseph Broadfoot said with such certainty it made Mack's heart skip a beat. Mack smiled weakly.

"Is that a fact?" Mack said teasing just a little at the sincerity of the boy's declaration.

"Uh huh," Joseph said, nodding his head up and down with a bounce. "Grandfather says so."

"Well then, I'm sure you will be a very big chief indeed someday," Mack said, meaning it more than he knew he could. This kid was a thief. He'd just stolen Mack Guthrie's heart as surely as if he'd reached his hand deep inside his chest and snatched it out, running off with it into the desert. *Stop thief!*

The boy lifted the medicine cup again and said only one word, "More."

Mack nodded and did as he was told, then laid his head back and let his eyes droop. He felt the coolness of the rag on his head again and the smell of herbs, flowers and something that reminded him of peppers. He heard Joseph's light little boy's voice sounding like it was disappearing off into the distance say slowly, "Sleep for a while, Mr. Mack Big Voice."

When Mack opened his eyes again, it could have been minutes or hours or even days and he wouldn't have known the difference. It had all been one great blur except for Joseph and the cabin. He still didn't know where exactly he was or how long he'd been there. But it didn't seem to matter so much anymore. He was warm and comfortable, no chills or fever to trouble him. It comforted him to look over and see Joseph sitting in a rocking chair over by the hearth. He wasn't rocking, just sitting with his head resting on one hand, staring into the fire. He startled when he heard Mack stir.

"Hello, Mr. Mack," the boy called out excitedly, skipping over to the bed.

"Hello, Joseph," Mack said, finding a little more energy to push himself up on his elbows to greet his young host properly.

"Are you feeling better, Mr. Mack? You look better," Joseph said, the seriousness in his eyes when he first saw him having long disappeared into his natural carefree child's shine.

"Yes, I am feeling much better, Joseph, and it's all thanks to you. It'll be good practice for the day when you become that big chief," Mack said, putting on exaggerated expressions for the boy's sake, enjoying more and more how he could abandon the *Sturm and Drang* of modern adult life and try to see it all through a nine-year-old's eyes.

"Are you hungry, Mr. Mack?" Joseph said excitedly. "I have some bacon and bread…and some soup and coffee."

Mack rolled over on his side and pushed himself up. He let his legs fall over the side of the bed and sat up. The inside of his head pitched around like the eye of a storm. His eyes fluttered and he quickly leaned back down on his side. Joseph went to him, searching his eyes.

"Mr. Mack, are you okay?"

Mack's head cleared at hearing the boy's voice, a steady swimming stoke back to shore. He was better. "I just sat up too fast, Joseph. Please, don't worry." Mack said and again, slowly this time and bracing himself more firmly with his hands, he sat up. He smiled widely for the little boy who had so much worry in his eyes.

Joseph smiled back.

"You can help me up, if you want to," Mack said with another weak smile.

Joseph rushed to his side as Mack put his feet on the floor, holding on to the bedpost, just in case. The boy stood close by and held his hand. Mack let out a great, deep, diaphragm sigh. It was the first real deep breath he'd had in months. He looked down, finally seeing the true measure of how small Joseph Broadfoot was compared to his own grown-man height.

Joseph looked back up at him thinking pretty much the same thing in reverse. *Wow, he's like a giant!*

Now feeling firm on his feet and with a clear head, he noticed that he was wearing an old-fashioned union suit, a big flannel shirt and thick white cotton socks like he'd seen in the old western movies. Seeing Joseph so small, barely coming to his waist, and trying to be so big, another of Autry's codes ran through his mind: *Be gentle with children, the elderly and animals.* He followed it and spoke from his heart. "It's not right that you should take care of me so much, Joseph. I'm a grown man, and you're just a little boy." He saw the boy's mouth open and knew what was going to come out. He jumped in before Joseph could speak. "I know. I know, you're gonna be a big chief someday," Mack said waving his hand and smiling just as wide as his face would allow. He couldn't stop himself whenever he thought of the first time his little big chief had said that.

"Uh huh," Joseph affirmed again with his bouncy nod.

"Well, I'm feeling better now. How about you let me take care of you for a while? Where's the kitchen?" Mack asked, giving the boy's shoulder a slight nudge.

Joseph giggled and led him to the half wall area over on the other side of the cabin. "Let's eat."

After dinner, they sat by the fire, Joseph in his rocking chair and Mack in a padded box chair. "Tell me a story, Mr. Mack."

Mack was taken aback. Was it a coincidence or did the boy know that Mack was a professional storyteller?

"What kind of story would you like to hear?" Mack asked, more than happy to oblige the little man who had apparently saved his life.

"A story about your life," the little boy replied.

"That's not really a good story for you, Joseph. How about something like *Peter Pan*?

The boy looked at Mack quizzically. "Peter Pan? Please, Mr. Mack, about you."

"Okay," Mack conceded, trying to find a way to make it honest. "There once was a man who had a very big name and spoke with…big words…"

"Big voice?" Joseph asked with an excited squeak, tying it in now with Mack's new Indian name.

"Yes, Joseph, Big Voice."

"But he was a very sad man," Mack continued, his voice taking on a softer, more reflective tone.

"Why?" the little boy asked innocently curious.

"Because for everything he had, lots of money, people pretending, telling him how big he is…but…inside he was very lonely,"

Joseph got a sad look in his eyes.

Mack tapped the heart-spot on his chest, then leaned over in his chair, letting his head drop into his hands so the little boy wouldn't see the wetness growing around his eyes.

"Don't be sad, Mister Mack…I'll be your friend," Joseph said instinctively, looking at him in rapt attention.

Mack wiped his face with the heels of his hands and looked up into Joseph's black marble eyes, wide and honest. Mack smiled tentatively. *Why you little thief, you*, he thought, but before he could say anything there was a sound, a loud scraping and banging over on the far side of the cabin, coming from the outside. Joseph jumped slightly. His eyes changed, now flashing with fear. The alarm in the boy's face made Mack angry. He didn't like seeing his little big chief afraid. It went against…*what?* The code. *Be gentle with children.* Mack wiped his eyes with the butt of his hands again and raised himself gingerly from his chair, shuffling sluggishly over to the side of the room where the sound came from. He reached out to the colorful red, black and white woven blanket hanging on the wall and pulled it back; a window. He had to crane his neck to see outside. The rain had stopped. The dark purple sky was lit with a netting of twinkling stars, but no movement, just the wind.

He let the blanket curtain fall back into place and turned back to the little boy. "There's nothing there, Joseph. It's okay," he said in a soothing tone and shuffled back to his chair. There was another sound, this time from the opposite side of the room, louder and more rattling, like rapid footsteps on a tin roof, echoing through the cabin interior. The little boy cried out and leapt out of his rocking chair. He was over by Mack's legs in lightning speed. He looked up at Mack, his eyes wild with terror; more than just a childish scare, real terror.

"Joseph? What is it? What's scaring you so? It's just the wind." Mack saw the tears well in the little big chief's eyes and he acted without thought. He reached down and scooped Joseph up onto his lap, holding him tightly under one arm. The little boy put his head to Mack's chest, pulling his knees up under his chin. "Please Joseph, tell me. What is it?" Mack pleaded with the frightened little boy. "What are you so afraid of?"

A little voice, timid and wavering came out, "The men," Joseph answered in a hushed, little-boy voice like he was afraid someone might hear him.

The answer made Mack even angrier, that someone could cause this fear is such an innocent child. "What men, Joseph?"

The boy shook his head, afraid to speak.

"Please, Joseph, tell Mister Mack who's scaring my little big chief."

The boy looked up into Mack's eyes, so filled with dread, struggling with what he didn't want to say to this man.

"Please," Mack coaxed gently again.

Joseph let his head hang down, such a weight on his little shoulders. He was embarrassed, ashamed to tell. He started to cry, burying his face in Mack's flannel.

"The white men," Joseph whispered with a sob.

Mack heard himself gasp, blindsided, the wind knocked out of him by the boy's response. "But why, Joseph? Why should you be afraid of the white men?" Mack pressed, holding Joseph closer and tighter, wanting to give him all of the security he knew how. Seeing that Mack wasn't going to be angry about what he'd said, Joseph relaxed a little, pulling his head back, wet eyed and looking into Mack's.

"Grandfather...says..." he slowly stuttered. "...I have to hide here. If the white men see me..." his voice started to hitch and he his breathing became rapid, "...they'll come take me away to the white man's school. Grand...father...says that they do terrible bad things to Indian children at the white man's school," and he started to sob into Mack's chest.

Mack's heart felt like it had been cleaved in two, emotion gushing out from the wound where his heart had been before it had been stolen by this little thief. His own eyes filled as he held the little boy close to him, rocking him slowly, gently humming, warmed by the heat and glow of the fireside, until they both nodded off, safe. *My little big chief.*

***

A wrenching tug, powerful hands yanked roughly at the bundle in his arms. The room was completely dark, pitch black. He couldn't see. He heard the cries as he felt himself being dragged from his chair to the ground, but he held on. He held on with all his might. A terrified child's echoing voice called out from the darkness as he felt the boy ripped violently from his arms.

'Help! Mister Mack! Don't let them take me! Ahhhhh, Mister Mack! Pleeeaaaasssssse, don't let them taaaaakkkkke meeeee awaaaaayyyyy," he heard Joseph's screams come out of the darkness. Mack tried to raise himself to his feet. He saw the open door of the cabin. He heard the heavy footfall of boots on the wood floor. Shadows moved along the wall as the boy cried out for him. "Don't let them take meeeee!" trailed off into the distance as the shadows passed through the door. He rose to his knees, crawling towards the sound of Joseph's hysterical cries. He saw the twinkling stars in the night sky and heard the sound of horse hooves as they pounded the wet desert ground. "Heeelllppppp meeeeee!"

He launched himself toward the door, but was struck from behind. His eyes went dim. He felt himself being gut kicked and rolled over onto his back. Someone was on him, straddling him, holding him down so he couldn't move. All he could do was cry out, pleading. "No! Don't…take…him! Don't take him!"

"Wake up, Mr. Guthrie, Wake up!" A man's gravelly voice came out of the darkness. Mack's eyes shot open, wet and bulging as he struggled under the man's grip. He saw a face, sun burnished red with a hatchet-like profile wearing a faded jeans shirt with a red bandana around his neck. The man turned to call out into the room. A curtain of long, straight black hair fell above Mack's bed as he fought to free his arms. "Big Jenny, hurry! His fever is breaking. Cool cloths. Big Jenny, help me!" the man's voice called out.

A few seconds later, Mack saw the pretty round face of a thick figured woman framed by long, black pigtails on each side, impish eyes and chubby cheeks with deep dimples, dressed in a vibrant colored zig-zag patterned tunic. He felt the coolness of damp cloths on his forehead and that smell again: herbs, flowers, menthol and peppers. He could see the man's eyes more clearly now and his face, eyes lined with crow's feet, deep ridges in his forehead and along his nose, coal black irises staring at him, clouded with deep concern, the long black hair now pushed back over his shoulders.

"It's alright now. The fever's broken. You've been a very sick man, Mr. Guthrie," a deep monotone voice came from the man.

"Where am I? Who are you?" Mack mumbled in a dry whisper, not knowing what was real anymore. The room seemed to breathe, the walls expanding and contracting before his eyes. He felt over his body and realized he was naked, soaked in his own sweat.

"My name is Hank Redfern. You're in my house. This is my cousin, Big Jenny. Do you think you can sit up?" the red man said, the monotone appearing to be his natural speech pattern. Mack nodded. He felt the man's hands on him again, helping him to sit up while Big Jenny gently pushed a soft pillow under him.

"How did I get here?" Mack croaked, his throat feeling swollen to the point of being closed.

"Here. Drink this first," Hank said, taking a pottery cup from Big Jenny and putting it in Mack's hand. Mack drank. He recognized that taste, honey and berries, sweet, sour and bitter.

"I found you on the highway two days ago. You've been unconscious, delirious. You really had us going for a while there, Mr. Guthrie," Hank said, now sitting calmly on the side of the bed with his hands folded in his lap. Big Jenny stood dutifully behind him, smiling sweetly and nodding.

"You know who I am?" Mack asked puzzled. Hank smiled, taking all of the menace out of his otherwise serious face.

"We do get *Time* magazine out here, Mr. Guthrie," Hank said, deadpan. The humor was all in his eyes, internally laughing with his first breath of relief that the white man wasn't going to die." We have cable television and Dunkin' Donuts, too," Hank continued, his monotone punctuated by a small, deep chuckle. "And if you were expecting me to say things like *heap big wampum teepee*? I'm afraid you'll be disappointed. They frown on that sort of thing at the University of Chicago," Hank went on, feeling so clever at putting the famous white man in his place, but inside still unwinding from the tension of the past two days, calming inside with the knowledge that his medicine had accomplished what he'd set it out to do. He felt a humming vibration in his front jeans pocket and reached inside for it, pulling out an IPhone. He hit a button and held it up to his ear.

"Sorry," Hank said. "Please excuse me," and he spoke an unknown language into the phone. "I have to go," he said rushing and grabbed a jacket from a chair. "Big Jenny will look after you until I get back."

"But...what about the boy? Where's the boy?" Mack coughed, the shrillness of his emotion lost in translation through his course, parched throat as he tried to raise himself hurriedly from the small cot. Hank was already through the door and didn't hear Mack call out, but Big Jenny did.

"What boy, Mr. Guthrie?" she asked shyly with a light almost childlike voice.

"Joseph. Joseph Broadfoot. The little boy who lives in the cabin in the desert!" he rasped loudly, his eyes bulging with urgency. "They're taking him away to a...school." Mack saw a startled, stricken look come into Big Jenny's otherwise placid, doe-like stare.

Big Jenny got up quickly and went to the small island countertop in the kitchen area. She picked up her IPhone and hit one button. Turning her head, she whispered into the little black box. Mack saw her nod as she listened to the voice on the other end. She spoke a few words with more nodding, then hung up.

A few seconds later she was over sitting on a low stool next to Mack's bed. She had a large painted bowl filled with water in her lap and a small brown bar of soap in her hand with a torn washcloth rag. She took Mack's arm and dabbed it lightly, then switched to long strokes. The smell of the soap, stinging and strong, made his nose tingle. He felt like he was laying on the shore of some far away beach, the tide at his feet, washing a little higher with each rolling wave, washing away his stress, his panic, his fear. Big Jenny started to speak, her light voice keeping an even conversational tone.

"My cousin is a very important man around here," she started as she wiped long lengths over his upper arm and shoulder. Mack just looked at her and listened, content to feel the strokes of the cloth and the smell of the soap. "He's a professor of anthropology," she said with a lilt in her voice, her tiny round eyes brimming with pride. "Heap big success," she said with a shy giggle under her hand, the dimples in her cheeks making her face glow.

Mack smiled back, the first since he met…Joseph. A tear came to his eye and rolled down the side of his face.

Big Jenny got up and took Mack by the arm, gently lifting him to sitting. She took his other arm and began to wash it. The warm water made Mack sigh out loud. "He's a medicine man, Mr. Guthrie," she said as if it were the most normal statement in the world.

It never even occurred to Mack to laugh or even smile. He just accepted it as one accepts the existence of nature.

"He healed you with his medicine," Big Jenny said softly as she washed Mack's back. She came back and sought his eyes. "My cousin has been under a great deal of pressure with his work, Mr. Guthrie; not enough money, no political support. He was having a failure anxiety attack when he found you in the desert. He says that the winds of the storm carry away the weight of his mind." Big Jenny got up then and went to a simple brown wooden dressing table at the foot of the bed. She came back with a large white rough cotton tunic, rolled it up and put it over Mack's head. She produced a comb next and drew it back through Mack's hair, then took the cloth and wiped his face.

Mack let his head fall back with his eyes closed, letting the hum of Big Jenny's voice soothe him.

"I have some beef broth on the stove. Do you think you can take a few sips?"

Mack nodded without speaking. A few seconds later, he felt Big Jenny's hand at the back of his neck. "Here, take a sip, Mr. Guthrie." He did as he was told. *Soooo gooood.* Salty, savory, closer to hot than warm, bits of green onion, small pieces of herbs. He took another long swallow, allowing the warmth of it slide down his throat, radiating through him like streams off of a big river into the rest of his body.

She left him with the cup and brought back a pair of faded brown canvas trousers, a pair of thick white cotton socks with red toes and a pair of fringed moccasins. "I'll go to the kitchen so you can dress," she said with a blush rushing up rapidly into her high, round cheekbones.

Mack did as he was told, no longer questioning anything, just grateful to be able to stand again and...breathe. The weight was gone from his chest.

Big Jenny came back a few minutes later with a sandwich in her hand—bacon and egg—and a steaming cup of coffee. "My cousin is trying to establish a historical landmark on the other side of town," she nudged as if she were leading him somewhere. *But where? Why?* She didn't bother to wait. Big Jenny's lips began to move, forming her words slowly and deliberately. "He's restoring the old Indian boarding school," she hinted. "It's a big job, Mr. Guthrie, lots of controversy. Things people would rather leave buried. He needs help," she said flatly without looking at him.

Five alarm fire whistles when off in Mack's head, shaking him out of his cloth-bath haze. Joseph's frightened little voice came back to him, "*...they do terrible bad things to Indian children at the white man's school.*" Mack's eyes filled. *Oh, my God!*

"Please take me there," Mack pleaded, putting his hand on hers. He had to see it for himself, and now. The spot where his heart used to be broke open and began weeping bitterly.

"Eat this first, keep you strong," she said handing him the sandwich and coffee, then went the cupboard closet by the front door. She came back with a heavy, quilt-lined coat and the hat he'd gotten from Ro Bodean.

They walked slowly, arm-in-arm down the dusty, dirt street on the edge of town. His eyes saw everything through the bright warm, morning rays as they warmed him with each step, the stiffness and aches flowing out of joints and muscles as they strolled, his body uncoiling until he could walk upright without much pain. Tin roofing atop mud brick houses and terra-cotta roofing on stucco buildings lined the outer streets off of the main road. Goats, chickens and dogs wandered aimlessly inside dried out wooden fences. The town was coming to life as they passed; women, some dressed like

Big Jenny, filled the streets with children, carts and bundles. Men in trucks headed out of town to jobs, a few on horses. Mack Guthrie found himself becoming hypnotized by the rhythm of it as he and Big Jenny moved unnoticed through the streets.

Soon they were standing outside of a large, abandoned building, weathered clapboard with two sets of windows on each side of a brown-stained double door at the front of the building. A larger annex building made of the same materials was set off to the back left. As they approached, Mack could see through the windows that everything on the inside was unpainted wood as well, the floors, the walls, the ceiling. He saw a wall-sized chalk board covering the upper half at the back of the room. He also saw signs of life. There was a workman on the back roof, a few women washing windows, some organizing of what appeared to be the contents of an attic or basement; large and small crates, antique steamer trunks, a few cardboard boxes, all coated with various layers of thick dust. Old-fashioned wood-and-wrought iron school desks were strewn along the walls leaving only a large wooden table in the center of the room.

Big Jenny opened the front door and motioned for Mack to go in. The women stopped what they were doing and maneuvered their way around the main room to the back of the building. Big Jenny called out something in her native tongue. Mack heard the sound of a man's heavy booted footfall. A shadow appeared from the back and Hank Redfern stepped through the doorway.

The two men looked at each other intently, Hank's black eyes betraying the depth of his sadness, Mack's eyes betraying the depth of his fear. They walked over to the table, a single wooden crate in the center. Hank reached into the box, pulling out an eight-by-ten, flat rectangle, handing it to Mack. "Smallpox...all of them that year," Hank said, his gravelly monotone voice overlain with sorrow, avoiding Mack's stare as he continued past him to join Big Jenny at the front door. They went out on the porch, leaving Mack alone.

Mack looked down at the photograph dated 1912. The building had a sign above the porch, Blackwood School. His eyes followed the rows of little Native American faces, none of them smiling. Names were written in white ink under each figure. His gut wrenched and his knees buckled, barely able grab onto the old table in time to keep from collapsing to the floor. He wailed out loud in grief to the empty room like a mortally wounded animal, clutching the photograph to the place where his heart used to be before it was so shamelessly stolen. *Joseph Broadfoot* was scrawled under his little figure.

"Grieve not, for our Joseph, Big Voice. We cannot change the past. It's only important what we do in the future," Hank said solemnly from the doorway in his monotone, the brightness of the sun behind him making his figure only a silhouette. He turned and shut the door behind him, leaving Mack alone with his little big chief.

"*Big Voice,*" a little boy's echoing whisper trailed on the air behind his ear, and from the back of his mind the words came forward, the DJ ol' Dusty's whisky voice like a white hot branding iron, Gene Autry's Cowboy Code emblazoning itself on his soul.

*A cowboy must. . .*
*Always tell the truth;*
*Be gentle with children, the elderly and animals;*
*Not advocate nor possess racially or religiously intolerant ideas;*
*Help people in distress;*
*Be a good worker;*
*Keep himself clean in thought, speech, action and personal habits...*

\*\*\*

"Whaaaatttt? Is he for real?" A high pitched man's voice said to a group of non-descript youngish men and women around a set of cloth-covered cubicles in the water cooler corner of the office. They were passing around a magazine: *Time*. Each made a mugging face of various natures. The photograph portrayed a man wearing a big, dark clay cowboy hat and dressed in a dusty earth tone rancher jacket over a worn jeans shirt, a faded American flag print bandana around his neck and a big square copper and agate belt buckle at his waist. He had a thick brush mustache and a four day scruff of a grizzled mix of brown and white, piercing, intense light green eyes, now burning fiercely defiant behind little round, gold-framed lenses. He had one hand on a holstered six-shooter on his left hip and was holding a little Native American boy on his right hip in front of the weathered gray wooden clapboard building. The cover read:

*Send Lawyers, Guns and Money:*
Mack Guthrie's *The Ghost of Billy the Kid*
takes Broadway by storm while the writer
takes on Congress, CNN and
the shame of the Indian Boarding Schools.

"Who the hell does he think he is?" Another of the young men at the water cooler asked with a snicker. "It's like he thinks he's Wyatt Earp, Marshall Matt Dillon and The Outlaw Josey Wales all rolled into one. He must have lost his mind, too much fire water and loco weed," he laughed at his own half-assed cleverness. "You can see it in his eyes. He's crazy," the young man said, making a whirling motion with his finger around his right temple.

"I think he's kind of hot," a tall blonde woman chimed in.

"Crazy like a fox," Ned Glassman said coming up on them from behind, catching them off guard goofing off. His associates turned quickly, embarrassed at being busted by the boss loafing and dissing their number one client. "His play has record breaking, advance box office sales. Everyone from Larry King to Oprah Winfrey is dying to interview him. He got Congress's attention, and people like us are talking about him at water coolers around the entire country," Ned lectured good naturedly with a firm slap on the back to his nearest associate as he walked away towards his own office. "Sounds like the old cowboy's hit the bull's eye if ya ask me."

*"Big Voice."*

## The End

## Note from the Author

The term **Indian boarding school** generally describes the many schools established in the United States during the late 19th century to educate Native American children according to western standards. By 1902, there were twenty-five federally funded, non-reservation schools across fifteen states and territories with a total enrollment of over 6,000. Although federal legislation made education compulsory for Native Americans, removing students from reservations required parental authorization which was often obtained by government officials through the use of threats, coercion and in some cases force, requiring parents to release a quota of students from any given reservation.

At the Indian boarding schools, the children were stripped of their ethnic and cultural identities (hair, clothing, etc.) and given English names. They were forbidden to speak their own languages and forced to attend Christian churches. Their lives were exclusively dictated by the strict control of their teachers which often included long hours of forced labor, grueling chores and severe punishments for non-compliance. This resulted in numerous documented traumatic experiences for many of the children who attended them (tragically, including emotional, physical and sexual abuse.) Infectious disease was also widespread and often swept through the schools due to inadequate sanitation and insufficient funding for meals compounded by a lack of information about causes and prevention.

The most telling statement on the philosophy embodied of the Indian boarding schools came from Captain Richard H. Pratt, founder of the notorious Carlisle School, based on an education program he had developed in an Indian prison who, in a speech in 1892 so famously said, "...*all the Indian there is in the race should be dead. Kill the Indian in him, and save the man.*"

# Nice, Little, Old...

***

*"I love those dear hearts and gentle people who live in my hometown.
I love those dear hearts and gentle people who never ever let you down."*

*Dear Hearts and Gentle People,*
Jim Reeves (1959)

***

J ust as Natalie Fisher pushed through the front double
doors of Old Dominion Retirement and Assisted
Living Village, another similarly dressed woman was
coming from the other direction. Both women were wearing
the modern-day equivalent of casual nursing wear; colorful,
patterned versions of doctor's scrubs with big white medical
coats over them.

"How'd it go today?" Natalie asked the other woman
rushing toward her.

"It was a little rough. We had three passings this
morning. Mr. Samson went first at 5:00 am, then Mrs. Coates
at 8 and Mr. Berensen at 9:45, but not enough hands on
board to handle it properly," Grace Leon replied as they
passed each other through the open doors. "No sweat now,"
Grace finished as she passed, "It's all done for the day, just
hope it stays that way till you get off at eleven."

Natalie worked her way through the sterile corridors,
made somewhat less so by the pastel-colored walls and
pictures of pastoral scenes hanging every few feet. Afraid
she'd be late she rushed down the last hall to the time clock
and the nurses' combination locker room and lounge. She
punched in quickly and threw her bag into her locker, then

rushed to the nurses' station to report in with the charge nurse.

"Boy, am I glad to see you," the busty, forty-something charge nurse, Rita Gonzalez, said as she saw the younger Natalie approaching. Just then an old man, slight and wrinkled to the point of seeming desiccation with only small tufts like cotton balls on the side of his head above his ears slowly began to pass with a walker. He lifted his walker up laboriously and put it down only inches away from where it had been, followed by the light shuffling sound of his slippered feet.

"Good afternoon, Mr. Ferrick," Natalie said brightly as if she were addressing a small child in the kind of voice that came naturally to those still with twenty-something energy.

"Good afternoon to you, too, Miss Fisher. Don't you look lovely today," the little old man said with a light coarse rasp to his voice and a kindly smile, showing that he had most of his teeth, still in good shape.

"Why thank you, Mr. Ferrick, what a nice thing to say," Natalie replied, smiling with a slight blush at the compliment.

The old man smiled again, nodding, then moved on, one strained shift of the walker followed by another shuffle of his feet until he had moved a few steps closer to his destination.

"What a nice little old man," Natalie Fisher said to Rita Gonzales.

"Yes, he's always so polite," Rita replied with a smile. "He's one of the real pleasures we have around here. Some of them can be so cranky and bitter. But, Mr. Ferrick? He's a real gem," Rita went on, rushing toward the combo locker-room and lounge.

When Natalie turned back to face the front of the circular desk, an old woman was waiting patiently for her attention. "Good afternoon, Mrs. Brownlee," Natalie said brightly again.

"Yes, good afternoon to you too, dear," the old woman replied smiling back. Dressed carefully in a lightweight pants suit made for women her age (which her chart read as being eighty-nine), Mrs. Brownlee always looked her best, hair, now all white and thin, always worn back in a bun with only the barest make-up to keep from looking like the death she had expected to come much earlier. Her eyes, a crystal blue, twinkled at the young nurse. "So how is that handsome fiancé of yours?" Emma Brownlee asked and patted Natalie's hand lightly, a knowing smile on her thin wrinkled lips.

Natalie blushed a little. She shouldn't have had her fiancé meet her at work. It made for some unkind comments from the guests and staff alike. He was big and handsome, of course, in a rugged sort of way, but more than a little older; old enough to be her father to be exact.

"He's just fine, Mrs. Brownlee," the young nurse nodded politely.

"Well that's good, dear. I'm glad to hear it. He seems to be quite a catch. I think you two make a lovely couple, no matter what others may think or say," the old woman leaned in slightly to whisper as if she were telling the girl a secret and patted Natalie's hand again as she walked away slowly in the same direction as the old man named Ferrick had gone; toward the day-room at the end of the hall.

*What a nice, little old lady*, Natalie thought to herself as she set about checking the charts for her next set of instructions. She had just gotten the charts arranged as she liked to work them when a tall, pale, cadaverous-looking man with black hair and watery green eyes in work casual clothes approached her from behind.

"Hello, Natalie," the man said, almost purring.

Natalie jumped away, startled. "Please, Brian, you creep me out when you sneak up on me like that!" the flustered young nurse said in a whispered shout, embarrassed by the fact that this slippery-looking guy seemed to have formed an unwarranted attachment to her. The hairs stood up on her arms. She rubbed it off and stepped back.

"We have a new client," he said and stepped sideways to reveal a small, wrinkled old man behind him. He had to have been eighty years if he was a day, liver spots all over his skin, hunched over and shrunken. "Natalie, this is Mr. Goethe. He'll be assigned to 110B until we can work out something a little more suitable. I understand we've had some vacancies this morning," slippery Brian smiled, revealing a smile that surprised her. If his voice weren't so creepy, his smile might have been attractive.

Natalie shuddered at the thought of it and shifted her attention to the old man. "Hello. It's so nice to meet you, Mr. Goethe. I'm sure you'll be very happy here," Natalie chirped like a spring robin at the pale, ashen-skinned octogenarian slumped before her.

He put out his hand. "Oh my, I'm sure I will be very happy, indeed," the old man said in a very practiced and affected English accent.

"Oh! And you're English. I think that's *so* cute. I just love your accent," the gullible young nurse squeaked at the old man, genuinely charmed by his stagey accent.

Mr. Goethe returned her smile, put out his hand and bowed. Natalie took the offered hand. Already halfway there, Mr. Goethe bent the rest of the way and gently kissed Natalie's hand.

"Charmed, completely, my dear," the old Englishman said, laying it on even thicker, his rheumy blue eyes betraying a spark of rare intelligence. Natalie giggled girlishly and reclaimed her hand.

"Well, let's get you settled in the day-room and introduce you to some of the other residents while I get housekeeping to make up your room," the young nurse said, once again, using her *talking-to-a-child*-like voice.

"That would be just lovely," Mr. Goethe responded and offered his arm to the young nurse like a true old school gentleman.

Natalie took his arm in return, then turned to the near-cadaver with the hot smile and said, "Isn't he the sweetest little old man?" more mouthing the words than speaking them.

A few minutes later they were at the set of double doors leading into the day-room. The large, comfortable looking room was dotted with small tables and scattered with chairs. Taking on the appearance of part game room, part living room, sofas were centered around what appeared to be two hubs of television views, different camps, mostly women with daytime soap operas on one side of the room, and men with The History Channel on the other. In the center wall opposite from the door was a large set of three plate glass picture windows with a lovely view of the outside and a few occupied chairs in front of it; *thinkers? Nature lovers?*

Mr. Goethe pointed to the panoramic view through the windows and the two figures seated before them. As they approached, Mr. Ferrick and Mrs. Brownlee turned to survey the newest resident, sizing him up. Emma Brownlee saw it first, that twinkle of fire light behind the rheumy blue eyes. Judd Ferrick saw it next. Mr. Ferrick and Mrs. Brownlee looked at each other wizened, knowingly then. She winked at him slyly. Just then, Nurse Natalie Fisher escorted Mr. Helmut Goethe over to the remaining chair next to the window and made the introductions to Mr. Ferrick and Mrs. Brownlee, then left the seniors to get acquainted, *Such nice little old people.*

Emma Brownlee looked sharply at the new resident, her eighty-nine-year-old eyes blazing with new interest. Her upper lip curled up in a sneer. "So whaddija do?"

Helmut Goethe's eyes came alive, glimmering as if a candle was burning behind each eye. "I molested close to three hundred kids, all under ten years old, that's when they're sweetest. I killed as much as half of them, it's hard to remember sometimes; so many, all over Europe and fifteen states, too, until I got prostate cancer ten years ago and had to get cut. What did you do?" His voice was as cold as steel, his English accent as sharp as a razor.

Emma Brownlee chucked and crossed her legs with a swing of her ankle. "I ran the rankest, stinkin' filthy whore house in New Orleans; girls, boys, kids, booze, drugs, guns, no rules, hundreds of them," the old woman seethed as if she were savoring a juicy piece of steak between her teeth. "And I made a fuckin' fortune at it from after the war until the Reagan era, lived like a queen all my goddamn life," she spat and waved her hand as if it were nothing. They both looked at Judd Ferrick then.

And you?" Goethe asked with an almost drooling smile, the definition of sinister coming forth on his almost a century old face at the other crippled old man with the walker.

"I poisoned my wife. Killed her for her money while I was fucking her sister. Then when I got tired of her sister, I killed her, too," Judd Ferrick groused through his teeth. They all had a good snicker as Helmut Goethe pulled up and sat in the chair nearest his new friends.

He had no sooner gotten comfortable in his new chair when his other new friend arrived, pushing a stainless steel medical cart made up to look like a tea cart. "I thought I'd have housekeeping make up something special for your first day here," Natalie Fisher said with a wide grin of self-accomplishment. The three new friends turned and looked up into her bright twenty-something clear eyes beaming out from her freshly scrubbed young face and thanked her sincerely and gratefully for their little treat.

Her good deed for the day done, Natalie scampered out back toward the door, leaving them alone again. Just as she reached the nursing station, she couldn't help but shake her head, thinking to herself with a smile, *What nice, little old people.*

**The End**

# BEYOND THE PALE

***

*"I have been ungrateful, I've been unwise, restless from the cradle.*
*Now I realize it's so hard to see the rainbow through glasses dark as*
*these. Maybe I'll be able from now on, on my knees.*
*Oh, I am weak. Oh, I know I am vain.*
*Take this weight from me, let my spirit be unchained."*

*Unchained,*
Johnny Cash (1996)

***

T he wake-up alarm went off at 5:00 am as it had
every morning for the last 5,565 mornings of his life
since he came to this place. Frank Jarrett opened his
eyes to the waking nightmare that had been his life since that
first day. A special fear squeezed his guts again, as it did every
two years on his special day. He sat up on his thinly padded
steel cot, letting his bare feet touch the cold, cement-slab
floor. His head dropped into his hands and he leaned
forward, resting his elbows on his knees. The feeling rose
from his gut and spread through the rest of his body like the
death rattle of snake venom, making his thickly muscled,
tattooed arms and back shudder with hopelessness. The guilt
and shame he had lived with every hour of every day for the
last fifteen years rushed over him like a massive tidal wave,
laying waste to whatever composure he had been able to
muster to raise his body to sitting.

He looked down at the gray concrete floor and saw two
heavy droplets of water as they fell from his face and landed
between his feet. It would take everything he had, and things
he didn't have, to get him through this day. He wiped his eyes

with the butt of his heavily muscled hands, thick skinned and calloused from fifteen years of intense, muscle tearing workouts in the yard, like the rest of his kind. Clad only in his boxers and tank tee, he stood up and moved toward the half sheet hung like a waist high curtain between the painted iron bars and the stainless steel commode. It was against the rules, but they were loosely enforced. Even the guards didn't want to watch them do their business and allowed them that small dignity.

He stood before the commode and listened to the sound of running water, never lifting his head to look into the polished steel bolted to the cement block wall that served as a mirror. He never looked at himself anymore, and when he did it was only to wash and shave, never acknowledging that there was a human being reflected in the steel looking back at him. It was like looking at a stranger. He had to convince himself that the reflection he saw wasn't really the Frank Jarrett he had once been—before he became a murderer—now unrecognizable with his shaved head and rock-wall features adorned only with a long western style, bright copper-colored mustache. It wasn't really him. It was a lead encased image he'd had to create for himself in order to survive.

The haunting of his soul had started in the early days of his life at Trenton State Prison; whenever he tried to look at himself, into his own eyes and saw the reflected image of Joe Brandon's face, the stark terror in his eyes as he pleaded for his life. "*Please don't kill me, Take the money, as much as you want but,*" he'd begged just before a twenty-five-year old Frank Jarrett, tweaked to the point of raging, animal insanity created by weeks of crystal meth running through his brain, pulled the trigger taking an innocent man's life for no better reason that to take the fifty bucks Joe Brandon had just taken from the ATM so that he could surprise his new wife with some Chinese take-out.

Frank heard the loud pop of the gunshot go off in his head and was jarred back into his current reality, finding

himself staring blankly into his own face, scarlet, bloodshot
eyes, long streams of wet guilt running down his cheeks. *I'm
sorry. I'm so sorry.* He let his head drop again, this time to
splash the cold water on his face. He had to get ready for the
day. He had no choice. It didn't matter that inside he would
have rather died than face another day living with a guilt that
he knew would never leave him alone. The shame of
remembrance that would follow his every thought and
movement like the grim reaper he had been for Joe Brandon
on that fateful night.

*Please kill me*, he begged silently inside himself. *I can't live
this way anymore.* He started to rock back and forth
rhythmically on his feet, his full black-and-white tattooed
arms clutching around himself as the only security he could
afford. There was the loud sound of a baton striking the bars
like a kid with a stick against a picket fence startled him out
of his small comfort. Frank almost jumped out of his heavily
inked skin.

"Wake up, Jarrett! You get a shower, remember? We
don't want ya stinkin' in there today do we?" the crew cut,
barrel-chested, blond guard called Todd laughed as the door
to the cell slammed open.

***

A hot shower and scrub always made him feel more
human. The hot water seemed to cleanse him for a little
while, the light bristles of the brush they allowed him seeming
to scrape off the layers of his dirtiness, his uncleanness…for a
little while. Withdrawing deeper into himself with each step,
two sets of footsteps eerily echoed as they approached the
steel reinforced wire-and-glass windowed double doors that
led to the dining hall, Frank took a deep breath. He was going
into an emotional overload, more than he was ever hard-
wired to handle. He withdrew even deeper, imagining that his
skin was no longer flesh but an impermeable alloy of high
tech metal, impervious to emotion, good or bad. *Feel nothin'!*

*You can't let yourself to feel nothin', boy, or it'll all come out of ya in a gushing river like a burst damn overlooking a thriving community, decimating everything in its wake, taking no prisoners.*

The muscle bound, light skinned black guard called Eustace hit a button and a buzzer sounded. There was a loud metallic click and the doors opened by themselves. Layer after layer he became that alloy, his shield growing thicker and thicker as he looked into the large, institutional dining hall. He saw row after row, table after table filled with the symbols of compliance, body after orange jump-suit-clad body lining each table as he was brought in. No one bothered to look up as he entered with Eustace close behind him. Or no one that anyone noticed.

A few seconds later and he was at his table waiting to feel the weight of the Eustace's hand on his shoulder signaling that it was okay for him to sit down, and as it is with habits of long standing, he robotically lifted one leg over the bench seat, then the other and sat, straight backed in his spot. Comforted by the still lingering feel of his temporarily clean body, he sat self-contained, pulling his body into himself as tightly as he could. He looked down to the tray in front of him; a so-called grilled beef patty, a clot of powdered eggs, overcooked, burnt potatoes with two pieces of toast, a cup of cold coffee and some powdered orange juice substitute. He didn't move, clinging to the limited security of his self-containment; a boxed unit of whatever was left of a human being.

He felt a slight nudge to his elbow, not aggressive or hostile, just slight, to get his attention. Frank didn't look up, but saw a big, pale hand pass over a white paper napkin wrapped object, leaving it on his tray. A napkin flap unfolded and he saw that it was another beefy patty between two pieces of toast. It made him look up, glancing around the table back and forth down one side then the other until he saw what he knew he would; Gunner Rasmussen's head, shaved of its thick, black hair, his bulging, tattooed neck bent over his tray. Rasmussen looked up, his crystal blue eyes meeting Frank's lashy green ones. Frank saw the softness in them that Gunner never let anyone else see. Rasmussen nodded slightly. Frank nodded back.

"Gun" Rasmussen had been his brother-protector since Frank had set foot in these hallowed halls. He couldn't explain it, nor did he feel the need to try. Gun had just taken a liking to him. And since he was the biggest, meanest most dangerous Aryan Brotherhood leader in the wing, from that day on Frank enjoyed the security of his person unknown to every other inmate. It was never questioned that no one, *absolutely no one* was to lay a hand in any form on the new fish unless he wanted to die horribly. Did he do *favors* for "The Gun"? Yes, of course he did, and even more, he didn't mind doing them.

Frank Jarrett had been unceremoniously born to a junkie mother who abandoned him before he was five years old to a life with an alcoholic, skid-row thief of a father who turned whipping his child into an Olympic sport. By the time Frank was fourteen, he was running the streets like a wild Indian on the war path, dabbling in drugs, shoplifting, but never enough to get him any time.

He barely made it through school, graduating from high school by the skin of his teeth with his only real incentive to do so being that he knew he could at least get a free lunch there. But also by then he was hopelessly entangled with the drug world, in his younger years acting as a runner for the dealers. But that was before he began using the product and finding that it was at least some escape from the beatings at home, the growls in his stomach during the nights and his endless sense of floating helplessly in a world where there was some new horror around every corner.

So when he entered Trenton State prison, he spent that first week huddled in the corner of his cell, never sleeping but waiting for someone to cut him, beat him, rape him or all three. But instead he felt the power and pressure of Gun's massive hand on his shoulder in the breakfast line on his eighth morning and heard his growling deep voice in his ear.

*"Stand easy, Bright Eyes. Nobody here's gonna touch ya. Trust me."*

Frank had looked up into Gun's eyes and saw something he'd never seen before in anyone, ever; a kindness, a sense of safety. Make no mistake, he knew what he'd have to do in exchange for that safety, and he was okay with it, because in all of his twenty-five years on the this planet earth to that point, it was the only time that he felt like he mattered to someone. So even though it was neither of their natures to be together, if it was a *bromance* that was required, it was a *bromance* that they would have going on from that point for fifteen years.

It was the only time Frank Jarrett had ever known the meaning of emotional intimacy with another human being. It was the only time he hadn't felt threatened or afraid and he accepted it like a drowning man clutches onto the tow rope that saves him. It just so happened that, for him, that tow rope turned out to be Gun Rasmussen, and he wasn't sorry. Because at least to Gun, Frank Jarrett was a man, a person and a human being, and for Frank Jarrett, Gun Rasmussen was the only respite from the never-ending crush of guilt for the crime he had committed that had brought him there; the senseless murder of an innocent man, one Joe Brandon, newlywed with his whole life ahead of him, and for what? Fifty dollars. Fifty stinkin' lousy dollars, hardly one single day's worth of drugs.

Under the patty sandwich in the napkin Frank saw what looked like pencil marks. He nudged the sandwich with his finger shifting it slightly, just enough to see the gray marks under it. It *was* pencil, letters in a mismatched, child-like printing. G L I L Y B E (*Good Luck I Love You Bright Eyes*). Frank looked up to the opposite corner of the table, to an empty spot at the end, then over to the doors. The guard was leading Gun away towards the doors.

*I love you, too.*

***

The large, white-faced clock with big black numbers ticked over to read five of nine as Frank was escorted through the hall to the waiting room. The broad-shouldered, black-haired guard called Hamilton pushed a series of numerically marked buttons alongside the door. The riveted, steel-reinforced door slid open. A small anteroom was lined on both sides by blue plastic chair seats over cheap aluminum legs bolted to the floor. There were six chairs on each side with a steel-reinforced hinged door at the other end. Three men were quietly seated on each side of the room; a few black, a few white, and few brown, all dressed in clean orange jump suits, white cotton socks and regulation black plastic sandal-like slippers.

"You know the drill," Hamilton said as the sliding door completed opening before them.

Frank went in slowly, keeping his eyes downcast, not wanting to stare at the others who he recognized from his long residence at Trenton. They were all there for the same reason, all sitting on pins and needles, their nerves shredded by the ordeal of waiting. The guard had been right. This was not Frank Jarrett's first time in this room, or even the second. This was his third trip down that long, cold hall and through that sliding steel door.

He took the seat in the corner farthest from the door he'd just come in through, struggling to maintain his composure and self-containment as much for his own dignity as for his inability to process the feelings assaulting him from every angle; the hopelessness of depression, the raging guilt, the conflict between knowing he deserved everything he got for his crime but still wanting the glimmering hope of another chance to start over, make good on his vow to live a good clean, quiet life on the outside.

But the conflict went even deeper than that. He was both afraid to succeed and be let out into a world with which he was no longer familiar, after having spent over half of his

adult life behind these bars, and leaving everything he had
come to know and feel comfortable around. Maybe it would
be better if he stayed. Then again he was afraid to be rejected,
to have the shameless carrot of freedom dangled cruelly
before his eyes, the hunger for it making him almost drool
with anticipation like an animal on a short chain, one that was
just that much shy of reaching that nice meaty bone, then
seeing it jerked away violently.

Since he had first become eligible for parole nearly six
years earlier, he'd come to this waiting room every two years.
Each time he relived the events that had brought him there;
the gunshot, Joe Brandon's face as he died, bleeding out on
the street as Frank snatched the two twenties and one ten
from his clutched hand, hearing Brandon's voice begging
again. He never really intended to pull the trigger. It was just
a nervous spasm caused by the drugs and the strain. He
couldn't even remember his brain sending the command to
his hand to pull. But that didn't change anything. Joe
Brandon was still dead and he knew he didn't deserve to be
free.

He deserved to suffer as long and as hard as it took until
he was dead and subject to suffering no more. He knew it
and owned it. There was no forgiveness for him and when it
was time for him to go into that room again and face that
panel of judging faces, he knew that all he could do was tell
them how he was a changed man, and that he knew he was
not worthy of freedom. He was certainly no threat to the
outside world, not ever again.

That special fear came up in his guts when he thought
about it. The idea of facing Joe Brandon's widow again,
seeing her pretty face and long dark hair pulled back so subtly
and hearing her light, sweet voice tell the panel how she had
been robbed of a life with her husband and that her son was
robbed of a father. It always made the panel gasp when she
tearfully explained how her husband had died without even
knowing that he was going to be a father. She'd planned to
tell him the night he was shot down. Frank could remember

how the tears flowed down her young face, only lightly made-up, as she struggled to say the words she knew she had to in order to keep that animal off the streets and from hurting other innocent people.

Frank's hands began to tremble slightly as he thought about how she spoke of her son being forever without a father, so not only was Jarrett's crime against her but also her son making it even more despicable. Frank had often thought that had it been just for herself, she might have met someone else and moved on with her life, but it was the boy that kept her coming to these parole reviews to make as sure as possible that the murderer Jarrett never saw the light of day again.

Panic grew in Frank's chest as he thought again about the second time she had spoken, only two years later. Her pretty face was showing signs of weariness as she explained how hard it was to raise her son alone and work to support him. He could remember as clearly as if it were yesterday, the shifting feelings as they flashed in her eyes as she spoke, anger, fear, loss, grief. He didn't want to go into that room with them, sitting there like a target with a bull's eye pinned to his chest for them all to take shots at him as he fought for whatever was left of his miserable life. But all the while the worst lurked in the darkness of his mind. He knew he didn't deserve his freedom. He knew that every word that woman had said was the absolute, unequivocal truth and that there would never be anything he could do to change that. Some men might be bitter and angry over her dogged refusal to let him forget. Others would blame her for their failure to be released, but not Frank Jarrett. He knew they were all right about him and what he did. He didn't deserve another chance.

His gut clenched and lurched forward with his breakfast. He kept it down, but he let his eyes fill. He couldn't think of any one single reason he could give that panel to grant him parole. Not one single good reason. *Please don't make me go in there again*, his inner, little-boy voice begged inside his head.

His feet started to shift and his knees started to bounce as the door opened and a tall, slender, brown inmate came out shaking his head and taking a seat over in the opposite corner. A thickly built, middle-aged woman with glasses held by a chain around her neck called out a name.

"Billy Brown," she called out to the room of orange suits. A short, wiry middle aged black man stood up and walked towards the door where the woman stood holding it open for him to enter, then closed it behind them both.

In the back of his mind just behind the mass of confusing thoughts, Frank heard the large white clock ticking the seconds away, *tick, tick, tick*. He looked up and saw it was nine thirty. Had that much time really gone by without him realizing it? He let his head hang back down, content to listen to the sound of the clock ticking away at his life, *tick, tick, tick*, until he found that in the deadly silence of that room that the sound of the clock ticking seemed to sooth him, *tick, tick, tick*, seemed to hypnotize him; a lulling comfort almost narcotic-like it its potency, *tick, tick, tick*. Time just slipped away from him. He let his eyes close and allowed himself to be absorbed by the sound, *tick, tick, tick*. He felt himself floating, so calmly and peacefully away from himself to somewhere else, somewhere safe and warm, a concrete womb of his own making.

He felt his body draw itself up closer, his head and chest leaning over, his knees drawing up closer to his chest, his arms held tightly within the space between them as the sound became the only thing left of his existence, *tick, tick, tick*. He didn't hear the door open again or see the wiry little man come out. He was long gone into his quiet, little cocoon, the only safely valve he had to contain so much of what he had been feeling but didn't know how to handle. Suddenly he heard a voice and the ticking stopped.

"Frank Jarrett," the woman with the chained glasses called out to the room.

Frank startled and was embarrassed to realize that his face was wet, his forehead was covered in beads of sweat and he was overcome by a chill that made him shake. He wiped his face quickly on his sleeves in embarrassment. The woman saw his distress and went over to him.

"Mr. Jarrett. It's time to come in now," she said quietly and touched his arm.

\*\*\*

"Please have a seat, Mr. Jarrett," a burly looking, dark-haired middle-aged man said with a motion of his hand from behind a long cafeteria table. His shirt was too tight around the neck, made all the more uncomfortable looking by his overwrought striped tie.

Frank took a seat in a chair placed at the far side of the table for that purpose; the *hot* seat. There was another smaller table, used for the witnesses or other concerned parties if they chose to attend and speak, facing the larger table further populated by a stylishly dressed and coiffed black woman to the left of the burly man with the desk plate in front of him reading, Mr. S. Barnes. The plate before the woman read, Mrs. H. Ellcott, and a third placed in front of the woman with the chained glasses reading, Ms. G. Arthur. Each of the panelists also had a small microphone perched before them to record the proceedings.

Frank sat silently waiting for what he knew he could expect; a recitation of the events of his crime, his time in, his behavior record. The burly man, Barnes, spoke again.

"Mr. Jarrett, we see here that you have maintained an exemplary behavior record here at Trenton State," and the man nodded his head in approval. Barnes had also been the chairperson of the panel on his last visit and worked to control how pleased he was to announce Frank's record. He had told Frank at the last hearing that he had high hopes for his future and still tried to believe that anything was possible if someone really wanted to change and find a new, better life for themselves.

"Thank you, Mr. Barnes," Frank nodded humbly to the man.

Frank dared for a brief second to look around the room, side glancing both ways without lifting his head. He held his breath. His heart beat wildly in his chest as he panned every aspect of the room in search of Melina Brandon's face. He didn't know what to think or to feel. He was just numb. He clutched at his own hands poised so properly in his lap, now white knuckled from the pressure. The room was empty. Where is she?

The stylish black woman, Mrs. H. Ellcott, nodded her agreement. She was new to his panel. She introduced herself first. "I'm Harlene Ellcott," the woman said with a smile, "and I agree with Mr. Barnes's assessment of your time here over the last few years. I see here that you got a vocational degree in auto mechanics while you were here. And an associate's degree in business," she said with a raise of her well plucked and penciled eyebrow. "Very ambitious, very commendable, indeed, Mr. Jarrett," Harlene Ellcott said, contemplatively leaning back in her chair, finding herself hoping against hope that every now and again, one success story would find its way out of their doors and into a functioning life.

Frank just nodded. He wasn't sure he could take all of their kind words of hope for him without bursting into tears. And that just wouldn't do for the hardened criminal that he was, now would it? *Jailbird!* The woman with the chained glasses, Ms. Arthur, looked at her watch and spoke next.

"We had notice from Mrs. Brandon requesting to speak here today, but it looks like," and she stopped. The visitor's door at the back of the room made a squeaking rush sound as the weather strip at the bottom scraped the floor. The room went silent as a small woman entered, thin and frail with a cane. Her head was wrapped in a dark green-patterned scarf that reminded one of leaves on a tree. Her eyes were covered by large black sun-glasses favored by the likes of a Jacqueline Onassis or a Maria Callas in the seventies. Her shoulders were covered by a matching green shawl over a black high-necked, long sleeve blouse and a long green-and-black-plaid wool skirt. She moved slowly, step by laborious step, the ten or so paces to the visitor's table.

"Mrs. Brandon?" Burly Barnes asked as the woman pulled the chair at the table out slowly, gingerly preparing herself to sit. She nodded.

"Yes," she said quietly, as if her voice became a wisp of smoke on the wind.

Frank Jarrett's heart dropped in his chest and he audibly gasped when he looked up at her and she saw him. He looked down again into his hands clasped so tightly in his lap, wringing the blood out of each other.

"Thank you for coming," Burly said once the woman seemed settled enough to continue. "I understand you've requested to make a statement for us to consider in our deliberations as to whether this board should grant Mr. Jarrett's request for parole."

The woman at the table nodded.

*Here it comes*, the little-boy voice in Frank's head said sadly.

The woman took off her dark sunglasses revealing her face and eyes to the board; ashen skin over delicate bone structure. Her eyes were sunken deep into their sockets giving the impression of large dark circles surrounding a pair of defeated brown eyes. She pulled a handkerchief out of her small black bag and dabbed her face and upper lip.

"My name is Melina Brandon. I was Joe Brandon's wife," and she hesitated briefly to collect herself. "Frank Jarrett, this man, murdered my husband fifteen years ago, cold bloodedly murdered him," and she turned the burning anger in her gaze on him. He didn't look up.

The woman's breath got rapid, her chest almost visibly fluttering with a rush of emotion. "Look at me!" she shouted at him, so solitary and vulnerable in his sad orange suit on a cheap plastic chair.

Frank raised his head on command and looked in her eyes. His own eyes filled to overflowing.

Melina Brandon wiped her eyes again then continued. "I'm dying, Mr. Jarrett," she said defiantly. Two voices on the panel gasped loudly. The third, Mrs. Ellcott, let go an "Oh my God."

"I have a malignant brain tumor that the doctor says will kill me before Christmas. Do you know what that means?" she screamed at him and slammed her hand loudly on the table top.

Frank jumped in his seat.

"That means that my son will be left alone in the world. You did that, Mr. Jarrett. Do I blame you for my disease? No, I don't," she said decisively shaking her head. "But at least he would still have had his father, but for you," and she broke down, pitiably crying into her hands.

Frank's eyes exploded with tears, a shower of them falling on his still clasped hands.

"I'm so sorry, so sorry," he cried into his lap, shaking his head, his heaving chest making his thickly muscled shoulders roll in waves over his back.

"Look at me, Mr. Jarrett," she said again determinedly, forcing Frank to raise his head. "There's something else I want you to know before I die." She stopped then and reached into her bag, pulling out a photograph. She motioned the guard to the panel table. "Please," she gestured with the picture in her hand. The guard took it and handed it to the panel. "This is my son. His name is Jacob. He's fifteen years old."

Ms. Arthur was the first to look upon the face of Jacob Brandon; fair and big boned like his father with auburn hair and a smattering trail of freckles across his cheeks and nose, hazel eyes brightly stared back from the school photograph. She passed the photograph to Barnes. He looked, shaking his head and passed it to Harlene.

"This is my son," Melina Brandon continued once she saw that the picture was in Frank's hand. "Fifteen years old, does that mean anything to you, Mr. Jarrett? I was carrying him while you were killing his father. But you know that already, don't you?" she asked and waited for his answer.

Frank nodded and answered simply and as respectfully as he knew how. "Yes," he replied in a hush.

"But then there's something you don't know. It was a very difficult birth. The stress of losing my husband caused me to have complications, severe complications, Mr. Jarrett. So when Jacob was born..." and her tears began to roll again, this time not angrily, instead soft sobs of sadness.

She stopped, wiped her face then started at him again. "It was a difficult birth, as I said. So difficult that Jacob was deprived of oxygen. Do you know what that means?"

Frank shook his head. He didn't know. He was an ignorant man.

"Do you know what that means?" she screamed at him across the room and burst into heart wrenching, unrestrained sobs.

Everyone in the room jumped and Frank the hardest. He cried again, out loud. It was as if her pain was all his, physically hurting him as he sat there. "No, I don't. I don't know," he wept and covered his face with his hands.

"It means that he will be no more than eight years old for the rest of his life, twelve maybe if he's lucky with a good school and a lot of hard work. He will never grow up to be a man, Mr. Jarrett."

"Oh my God," Gale Arthur said crossing herself subtly and reaching into her purse for a hanky.

"Because of you, Mr. Jarrett. Because of you, my son will be a child forever. His father is dead. I am dying and Jacob will be left alone in a world that will tear him apart. Joe's parents are dead. My father ran off when I was a baby, but then you know what that's like, don't you? Yes, I know who you are. I know where you come from," she said never taking her glaring, shiny wet eyes from his face. "My own mother is old and not well herself. Who is going to love my child, Mr. Jarrett? Who's going to protect him from all the terrible things that can happen to him? A foster home? Some state mental institution? No, Mr. Jarrett, not for my son. So I'm going to tell you who is going to love him, look after him and protect him. You are, Mr. Jarrett, if you ever expect to get out of here; if you ever had any real hope for redemption and forgiveness. You will do this for him."

Behind the panel table three mouths dropped open in abject shock and astonishment by what they'd just heard. Harlene Ellcott was the only one able to form words. "Oh, this is beyond the pale," she said in weepy exasperation, wiping her eyes in her finely embroidered lace handkerchief.

"Mr. Jarrett, I want you to adopt my son, make him your own after I'm gone and when you look in his face every day, into his eyes, I want you to remember how he got here and what you did, and do what's right by him. Be a man for him and protect him for as long as you draw breath on this planet. For the rest of your life and his, and most of all, you'll do everything in your earthly power to make him happy. It's your only hope, Mr. Jarrett." With her last statement, her breathing became more rapid and she stood at the table and began to turn. Her knees went weak and she had to grab onto the back of her chair to steady herself. Burly Barnes wiped his nose and motioned with his hand for the guard to go to her.

"Help her. Help her," he said flustered and blew his nose lightly. The guard was over by the woman in a flash, gently taking her by the arm and leading her toward the door. Halfway there, she stopped, turning slowly and swallowing before she could speak. She looked at Frank Jarrett, quaking to the core of his being in that cheap little blue plastic chair.

"I've arranged for you to have a job at a local auto body shop. You'll live with my mother and be supported by a trust I've set up with the benefits of Joe's and my life insurance."

Frank raised his head, his eyes made almost invisible by the weeping-induced swelling surrounding them. Melina Brandon then turned her attention to the panel. One last look and she turned to go, passing through the door like a ghost into the gray mist of an evening fog.

***

Eustace's big sausage fingers rapidly tapped the numeric code into the little door side box on the wall and the barred door popped open. They walked through and out into the sunlight, just a few more feet before they were at the last door to the outside world, another barred gate set into a high brick and mortar wall.

"You gonna be alright?" the guard asked trying hard not to give away the well of emotion he was feeling at sending another one of his hopefuls out into the world again with little more than a wing and a prayer.

"I guess I'm gonna find out," Frank replied smiling weakly, scared to death but even more scared to admit it to anyone. He was dressed in street clothes for the first time in fifteen years. They felt strange. The big plaid flannel shirt felt so soft against his skin. The new jeans they'd gotten for him were right off the shelf, still stiff and deep indigo blue and his new sneakers were blindingly bright white. Eustace gave him a good firm pat on the back and handed his bag over to him, nothing much in it, almost nothing in fact after not having anything of his own for over fifteen years.

He put his hand out to the guard and shook it hard. "Thanks for everything, Eustace," he said sincerely, struggling so desperately to keep his breathing even and his forehead and upper lip dry. He hesitated. Eustace saw and came up behind him, speaking softly over his shoulder.

"Just take it one step at a time, man, one day at a time. You'll be fine. I have faith in you," and he gave him a slight nudge through the open gate to the street. Eustace slowly closed the gate behind him and disappeared back behind the wall, leaving Frank Jarrett out on the street, alone for the first time in fifteen years.

Frank's eyes could hardly take it all in, scanning everywhere. The world was all so big, so tall, so loud, so overwhelming. His head started to spin a little so he brought his eyes back down to street level. There was an old Jeep

Wagoneer with wood paneled sides at the curb and an older woman was standing in front of it, small and thin with a mass of wavy gray hair, wrapped tightly in an oversized cardigan sweater against the cold December wind.

She had a boy next to her, tall for his age and big boned. The boy saw him and broke into a lumbering trot like an oversized golden retriever pup, bounding towards him and knocking over the furniture. *How did that happen?* He stopped short in front of Frank and looked up at him, clear round hazel eyes staring up at him, freckled and rosy cheeked.

"Are you Frank?" the boy asked innocently. Frank nodded.

"Yep. Uh huh,"

"Grandma says you're gonna be my new dad," Jacob said like it was the most common thing in the world. "Is that true?"

Frank nodded again and before he could say another word, the big boy threw his arms around Frank's waist and hugged him tight.

"I'm glad," Jacob said excitedly. Frank didn't know what to do, how to respond. For a second he froze, then raised his arms, stiffly, awkwardly at first and put them around the boy, hugging him back tightly. One hand went up, to the top of the boy's head; a light, loving stroke against his hair.

"Me, too."

## The End

The following are excerpts from K. Patrick Malone's
most recent multi-award winning novel

## The House At Miller's Court

and his horrifying debut novel

## INSIDE A HAUNTED MIND

# The House at

# Miller's Court

## Chapter One
## Defining Moments

The black Jeep Cherokee drove up the winding, hilly road. He could see the upper level of the large institutional looking red brick building as it rose higher; more and more of it above the sea of tree tops before him as he drove towards the crest of the hill. A few more minutes and he was at the driveway, turning in and pulling into a parking space facing away from the now huge building. George Lathero turned off the engine and sat there, Katy Perry's voice coming out of the dashboard radio, *Shut up and put your money where your mouth is. That's whatcha get for waking up in Vegas,* letting his head hang low as he thought about the unknown world that he was about to encounter.

He raised his head to look into the rearview mirror and saw the red brick-and-mortar expanse behind him. He looked higher and saw the large white letters in reverse in the mirror's reflection, but he knew what it read, and it made his heart drop into his stomach: *Baltimore County Corrections.* He felt his hand on the door handle and willed it to pull open, then slowly got out of the truck feeling like his feet were lead and his heart an even heavier metal.

As he took in the sight of it, he noticed a line of people stringing out of the entrance. Dreading what he was doing, he approached, appearing to those in the line that he was exactly what he portrayed; a man out of his element.

Lost in his thoughts and his head still hanging low, George heard a voice and looked up. Three girls were smiling at him. "Hey, Mister. You lost?" the tall, thin black girl in the center with big gold hoop earrings laughed. The other two, a chubby white girl with long stringy hair and a baby stroller and a short and even chubbier dark girl, looked him up and down; part suspicious, part amused.

"Are you a cop?" the chubby white girl asked looking nonchalantly back into her *Mother's Monthly Magazine*. George hesitated at first, taken aback by the question. He must have looked it because before he could respond, the even chubbier black girl jumped in.

"Relax, Mister. She's just kiddin' ya. It's just that you look so…well…straight."

George stood for a moment and flushed, thinking about how these girls must see him; tall and a little beefy but still well built, clean shaven with the tail end of a summer tan from being out on the playing field so much. He was the Director of Athletics at the University of Maryland after all, and a former career athlete himself. He always kept his dark brown hair short, only now going gray at the sides at forty-three years old. And he was wearing a light blue cotton oxford shirt with khakis and white sneakers. *What else would they think?*

He smiled, giving the girls their due and shook his head; a little embarrassed but feeling not so alone anymore. "I've never done this before," he said as shyly as George Lathero ever got. He wasn't the shy type. It wasn't his nature, but right then, at that moment, he was so far out of his own safe little world that he didn't know what else to do.

The girls smiled back. "Don't worry, Mister. We'll get ya through it," the chubby black girl said kindly. "We just wait here in line for our fifteen-minute visit. They take us in twenty at a time. It's all the booths they have," the chubby white girl said with a voice of authority, not lifting her face out of the magazine.

"But they'll run your driver's license to see if ya got any warrants out on ya. So if ya do, ya better turn now and go...very quietly," the tall black girl with the earrings chimed in, pointing a long red fingernail with a daisy appliqué on the tip at him.

George figured whatever he was doing was working with the girls, so he kept it up. "Thanks, I really appreciate this, ladies," he said taking a deep breath and putting his hands in his pockets.

The chubby black girl's eyes got wide and she started to fan herself with her hand. "Ooooooohhh, child," she said, making like she was going to faint. It went completely over George's head until they were at the door and going through the metal detector. She went first, then turned to George, looked him in the eye and said, "Mister, I'd call you Big Daddy, a-n-y-t-i-m-e," then giggled her way off with a twitchy waddle to check in with the guard.

⌗

Sitting alone and waiting his turn, George thought about where he was and how he was to say what he had to say, or even if he should say. The next sound he heard was the booming voice of the big, late-middle-aged guard posted at the door leading to the visiting stalls. "Lathero!" the guard called out loudly. George stood up, almost on command, reminding him of the dozens of coaches calling out his name over his almost thirty years on a playing field of one kind or another. The guard waved him over and opened the door to the unit, leaving him facing a row of ten stalls divided by thick plexi-glass sheets with five-inch holes in the centers covered by perforated metal grills.

"Number eight, pal," the guard called gruffly out behind him.

George headed toward the stall with the large black eight over it and sat down on the stool, waiting. He saw a line of orange coverall-dressed men come through a door at the back accompanied by a large, dark-black guard at the front and a thinner red-headed guard at the back.

Once all the men were in the room, the large black guard waved his hand. The line broke formation and the men went to their respective stalls. From the back George saw what he was dreading; a tall man, his dark brown hair all askew, not as built as George; slighter and more sinewy, and looking bad, woeful, head hanging.

When the man lifted his head, George Lathero's heart broke and he wanted to cry. His baby brother, Will Lathero, the kid he taught to read and ride a bike, play baseball and use protection looked back at him through tired eyes underscored with sunken dark circles; unshaven, underfed, so pale and scared. Caged like an animal. "George!" Will rushed to the stall and sat down, putting the palm of his hand up flat against the glass. George automatically did the same, choked with emotion; fear, anger, worry, frustration.

"I hate seeing you in here," he blurted out emotionally as the color came up his neck into his face.

Will let his head hang. "I'm so sorry, George. I didn't want you to find out. I called Jennifer but I could never get through." Then the dawn of realization came into his eyes. "She called you, didn't she?"

George nodded.

"Is she coming? Is she outside?" Will asked anxiously, his bloodshot eyes searching George's. George just shook his head, working to find the words to say what was coming next. Will came closer to the glass, his green lashy eyes dark with intent. "George, talk to me, please," Will begged, his mouth almost touching the steel voice grill. George looked up, searching his brother's eyes that were so much like his own and their mother's, and spoke slowly, haltingly.

"She's...not coming, Will," George said sadly back into the perforated hole. "She called and told me...that...she packed all of your things and put them in your truck. She told me she'd leave the keys in her mail box and that I should come and get it, so I did. It's over at my house, our new house."

Will and George's eyes filled at the same time as they looked at each other. Will was the first to look away, down at his hands folded in his lap.

George put the palm of his hand back up to the glass. "Will, everything will be alright," he said quietly.

Will didn't bother to look back up. He just spoke sadly. "George, I've already lost my job over this. I have no money and no place to go when I get out. I don't know what I'm going to do," and he put his hands up to his face to wipe away the wetness.

The college-aged George Lathero rose up in him again, reminding him of the time he had to take on three high schoolers to keep Will from getting his ass kicked over some girl when he was sixteen. He was and always had been his brother's keeper from the day he was born, and George Lathero did what he always did when it came to Will Lathero. His wordless, unspoken mind shook out the bright blue superhero cape that lay dormant in the unacknowledged parts of who he was since his earliest memories, revealing himself as able to leap tall buildings in a single bound when called upon to...save the day? Silent trumpets blared behind his eyes to the sound of the Mighty Mouse cartoon theme song, *Here I come to save the daaaay!*

"Will, please, don't worry, and no lectures. I promise, not now. Renee and I just bought a new house, a big one. Really big; big enough for you, too. I'll pick you up when they let you out and you can come live with us until you get back on your feet. I'll take care of you, Will," then hesitated until he had Will's full gaze. "Don't I always?" George asked, no longer able to keep his full eyes from overflowing or caring if he did, because as he looked through that glass, Will was five years old again, scared to death to start school and the ten-year-old George was the one to walk him every day and meet him when school was done while their parents worked. George put his palm back up to the glass. Will did the same, wiping his eyes with his other hand.

"What would I ever do without you, George?"

⊣⊔⊢
⊓⊓⊓

Renee Lathero put her feet up on the kitchen table and took a deep breath as she stared at herself in the shiny metal of the toaster on the counter not far from her. Her naturally flirty blue-green eyes stared back at her. *Is that what did it for you, George?*

It had been a long hard week of struggling valiantly to put the house together into some semblance of livable order the best she could in a short time. There were boxes to be unpacked, the painter and curtains to deal with, and a nonstop rush of cleaning at every turn. It helped that George took a week off from work to do most of the lifting and shifting of the heavy furniture and crates, but time was running out. Her mother had already closed on her condo and would be arriving at the new house in a few days. But what a god-send she would be, adding ten thousand dollars to the down payment on their new place and her presence living there with them to help look after Robin while Renee looked for a job and hopefully went back to work.

She took another deep breath and a sip of her tea. At thirty-six, she felt like she wasn't getting any younger after the experience of packing up George's house and then her own so they would all be ready to move into the big house at once. But it was a good ache and a good tired. She finally had everything she'd always dreamed of since she was a young girl; a wonderful man to love and who loved her back, a secure home for her son, finally being able to reconcile with her mother after more than a few years of estrangement, and now this big beautiful old house with room enough to breathe, live and love as she'd always wanted to all her life. What else could a girl ask for in life? *Nothing*, Renee Lathero answered herself silently with a satisfied smile. But there was still so much to do, from contact paper on the many-shelved closets, to choosing carpet, wallpaper and other household items (for which her mother would gratefully help out). *Thanks, Mama.*

She pushed her lightened, shoulder-bobbed blond hair out of her face and took another sip of tea, thinking back on how this all happened and so fast; only eighteen months since she met the then infamous George Lathero. *"The most eligible bachelor in all of Woodbury, Maryland"* her friend and neighbor Marata had said when they saw him the night of Woodbury High School's graduation ceremony.

She had been feeling rather off her mark for a long time, twelve years to be exact since her husband was killed in Desert Storm. They were just kids when they married. He was twenty-four and she was twenty-two and had just graduated college when Joseph Delcore proposed to her.

They'd met during her first year in college. All of her friends thought it was so romantic. He was young and handsome, dark Italian background and ROTC. But romance turned to reality when Joe went off to Desert Storm and she got the notification that she was a widow before she'd reached her sixth month of pregnancy.

It was the start of the rift between her and her mother. *"You're still a beautiful young girl, Renee. Find another man and quick. You have a child to think about now. Don't be so selfish,"* Vivian Crane had said to her daughter before she'd even had time to grieve or recover from the difficult birth Robin had given her. *"You mean like you did, Mama? Over and over and over again?"* Renee had snapped back, referring to the fact that her mother was on her third husband by then, divorced one, buried one and was on her third which lasted until he died. Then she went on to divorce another before she was fifty-five.

Out of both spite against her mother and to prove that she could make it on her own and her overprotection of her baby son, Renee dated very little during the twelve years of loneliness before she met George. The men she did date seemed to be so common, only after her ass, not wanting the responsibility of her child. So she concentrated all of her energies on working as a legal secretary to support herself and

Robin, struggling to raise him right in a world that she knew would try and shit can him; just another latch key kid.

As she sat there in her new house, her new kitchen, and settling into her new life, Renee MacDowell Delcore Lathero thought back to the time she was rushing through a thunder storm to get Robin to the emergency room with a fever late one night when he was only four. The car stalled on the highway. She'd turned the radio on to try and calm herself until the police got there and heard an old song from the seventies; Helen Reddy singing *You and Me Against the World*. And she fell to pieces.

Then in that twelfth year, she'd reluctantly agreed to go with her crazy neighbor, Marata, to her daughter's high school graduation ceremony and the block party afterward. It made sense at the time since it would only be two more years before Robin would be going to high school, so she might as well look the place over. And Marata was always a blast and so much fun to be with.

They were in a middle row when the principal called out Marata's daughter's name and she'd glanced over to the left front row and noticed a man leaning anxiously forward in his seat. He was very handsome in an all-American sort of way, clearly an athlete of some sort. He had that look, very coach-like with a whistle dangling from a lanyard around his neck.

Renee heard the principal announce another name, *Drake Lathero*, and saw a well built, smiling blonde teenager move across the stage waving to someone in the audience. She heard the riot of shouting and clapping from that front left row as her all-American leapt to his feet, whistling, stomping and making a scene. The look of pride on his face as he carried on for the boy who she assumed was his son made Renee tear up. She could tell that this graduating boy, Drake, must have been that man's whole life, just like Robin was hers and she found herself somehow so moved by it. It also didn't pass her notice that there was no woman standing or sitting next to him, clapping or otherwise, just an old man on one side and another, middle-aged man on the other.

She could almost feel that elbow to her side again as Marata caught her staring. Marata leaned into her and quietly whispered those now famous words. *"That's George Lathero, The most eligible bachelor in all of Woodbury, Maryland,"* Marata had said with a saucy smile. Renee blushed. Marata went on. *"No women in his life, not ever. He's been raising that boy all on his own. Rumor has it that his wife left him when the boy was still a baby, wanted a career or some such nonsense."* Then Marata winked at her, her dark eyes shining with mischief. *"Rumor also has it that he may be* Father Knows Best *within a hundred miles of his son, but outside that hundred mile limit he gets up to being quite a party boy when he goes away for his conventions. He's the Director of Athletics over at the University. I also know that Drake'll be going away to college in the fall so George will be...well...all alone again,"* Marata finished with another sharp elbow to Renee's side.

Renee blushed furiously and gave her friend a sharp elbow back, flashing the smile that saw her voted *"Most likely to blind the boys,"* under her high school graduation picture; the one that her mother never failed to remind her where it came from whenever she thought her daughter was getting too uppity. *"Where do you think you got your looks from, Renee, a sack of grits? You got 'em from me, Baby, hair, eyes, smile...and your downright uprights. All of it. Came from me,"* and she'd laugh because even at the ripe age of sixty-one, Vivian Ainsley MacDowell Simpson Argyle Crane was still one hell of a good looking woman.

After the ceremony was over and everyone was rushing to get out of the auditorium to start the block party next to the building, Renee felt a strong tug on her arm. Marata pulled her back to wait and watch as George Lathero walked toward the exit, excitedly pushing and tugging, hugging and rough-housing with the good looking blonde teenager she saw on stage before the riot started. The man was so proud of his son. It splashed all over him like front page news and, once again, Renee found that to be so...attractive; the ease in the way he walked and the way he handled his son, rough and manly but still loving and honest... healthy...shining.

She heard Marata's voice whispering again in her ear as

they watched him. *"I don't know about the first rumor about his wife, but I'm inclined to believe the second one. Don't be fooled for a minute by that lily white and uptight look he's got going on. I saw him throw down at the graduation dance a few nights ago and, girl! Funky and funny! Embarrassed the shit out of the boy but you shoulda seen the wind that was blowin' through the skirts watching him. I saw him at the Shop-Rite the other day, too, in his tight little tee-shirt and cargo shorts, wearing some cute flip flops."*

*"Alright! Alright! I get it, Marata,"* Renee whispered back through her teeth. *"George Lathero is 'the man',"* she said, exasperated.

*"Play your cards right, sweet cakes, and he could be your man. And his son IS moving out to go to college in September. Poor lonely George,"* Marata said, putting on her 'oh woe is me' voice. *"Hell, if I were into white boys, I'd go after him for myself,"* Marata said, bumping her slimmer-hipped friend with her more than ample rear, laughing and dragging Renee to playfully follow him as they walked a respectable distance behind *the man,* suppressing small, school girl giggles as they watched the way his aging athlete's ass went from side to side when he walked.

Outside the block party had started. The street was blocked off at both ends; the exhilarating sound of arena rock music coming from the end farthest away from them. On their way into the thick of it, Marata's daughter, Martika, joined them, fitting herself in between the two grown women; taking them arm in arm to the drink tables, then over to the food tables. Renee could almost smell again the acrid smoke that signaled that the barbequing had begun.

Alone again, the two women, abandoned by Martika to join her friends, wandered through the crowd eating leisurely from light plates of food, salads and grilled chicken fingers; chatting about the most mundane of subjects. More than being two youngish women on their own, Marata had another daughter the same age as Renee's Robin; both twelve and just getting to the point where they were beginning to ask the tough questions.

Since Marata knew her way around and Renee had never

been near the school before, Renee felt comfortable letting Marata lead as they walked around until Marata suddenly stopped, seeming to dally and dawdle in one spot as she seemed to chatter in a rapid, high-pitched pace. The next thing Renee knew, she felt a forceful shove at her elbow and let out an involuntary squawk as she saw her plate fly from her hand and land over her shoulder, accompanied by the sound of a man's deep voice. *"What the...?"*

She turned around quickly to see her potato salad, cole slaw and leftover barbeque sauce sprayed like abstract art all over the front of George Lathero's starched pale green shirt. Stunned, she looked up and saw his face; abject shock as he looked down at the front of his shirt. He looked back up at her, smiling, rebounding like the George he had always been. He took his finger and swiped some of the barbeque sauce off of his shirt and stuck it in his mouth, then looked at her and said, *"Mmmmm. I was meaning to get over there and try some of that. Now I can save the trip,"* and he laughed out loud.

From there, she did everything her mother had taught her. Followed her instructions to the letter without even realizing she was doing it. *"Always be a lady, Renee. And remember, no matter what men say, a lady always wins the day."* She apologized profusely; feeling like she wanted to crawl into herself with embarrassment at first, but when she heard him laugh that deep man's laugh again she couldn't help but laugh with him. With no conscious thought, her lashes were batting, her voice got flirty and she did her best to try and remember how to smile the smile that "would blind all the boys." The next thing she knew she was sounding like her mother and inviting him back to her house to wash his shirt for him, and to her complete surprise, he accepted.

For George's part, he thought himself lucky to have been within reach of that flying plate. It made him feel like he'd fallen back more than twenty years to when he was a star quarterback in college. *"So you want to be a football hero,"* seemed to play in the back of his mind as he looked at Renee. He got butterflies in his stomach and felt like he wanted to start kicking at the ground and shrug his shoulders like he was twenty again. He had been so lonely for something more than just sex with convention girls for so long. And there was something different about this one, oddly both naughty and nice. Naughty in the way there was just a little bit of lace camisole showing through the top of her summer white sweater blouse accentuating her clearly perky breasts; nice in the way that made him think how much he'd like to walk down the street holding her hand and have everyone see it.

When they got to her house, he walked her to the door like a gentleman. God, she was so nervous she dropped the keys to her front door. He picked them up for her accidentally touching her hand. *What should I do? Should I ask him in...for coffee...to meet Robin? What? What?* Before she could choose a course of action, the decision was made for her when her front door opened and she saw old Mrs. Bayless' face. *"Oh I'm so glad it's you, Missy. I got scared there for a minute when I heard the noise,"* the old lady said, curiously giving George the once over.

The old lady had known Renee and Robin for years and knew it wasn't like Renee to bring a man home...ever. But when she saw the large blotchy stain on the front of George's shirt, she smiled. *"Had a little accident there, Missy?"* the old woman said, opening the door fully to let them in.

*"Mrs. Bayless, thank God. It was my fault. Can you help me with this?"* Renee whispered in the old lady's ear as she passed her in the doorway.

The old woman smiled and took the situation in hand. *"I'll take that shirt, Mister...?"*

*"George, George Lathero,"* he nodded to the old woman as he came into the entry hall and started unbuttoning his shirt.

*"Why don't you take Mr. Lathero in the kitchen and put on a pot of coffee, Missy, while I take care of this?"* the old woman said but was thinking, *It's about time you took the jewels out of their case, Missy, and it looks like you pulled a winner this time even if you did have to dump your dinner on him to do it.*

*"Mrs. Bayless, I could kiss you,"* Renee said and pointed to

the kitchen. But before they could turn to go, they heard the light shuffling sound of bare feet on the stairs.

George looked up to see a young boy standing on the landing halfway down the stairs in faded, wash-worn flannel pajamas with some sort of cartoon characters on them, average height for a boy his age but slightly built with olive skin. The boy had short, tousled hair the color of black coffee with matching eyes, huge with long black lashes and features more narrow than broad that told of Andalusian Spain or Sicily. The image that came to George's mind was of a lost young buck deer.

*"George, this is my son, Robin."*

Triggered by the thought of the first time George met Robin, Renee came out of her comfortable haze and was back in her new kitchen. Her tea cup was empty and her legs numb from being so high up on the table. *Robin!* She hadn't heard a peep out of him for hours and even though he was fourteen now, she still had that mother's instinct flowing strongly enough through her to want to know where he was and what he was doing at every turn.

She got up from the table and ambled, numb legged, through the swinging kitchen door, calling out to him. "Robin! Robin! Sweetheart, are you upstairs?" No response. She looked at the clock. It was 4:30 p.m. and the late summer sun was still high in the sky. She walked to the side back door feeling her legs come back to life and called out back for him. "Robin!" No response.

Not particularly concerned, she slipped on her sandals and went out the back door, walking towards the left of the house where there were three tall old oak trees. Knowing her boy as most mothers do, she knew that she'd most likely find him under a tree with a book. If she had to guess, it would be one of his boy's adventure stories: pirates or one of Rudyard Kipling's stories of India. He loved those.

As she got closer to the trees, she could see his gangly bare legs and his feet in his worn out old black Converse All Star sneakers sticking out from behind the foremost tree.

"Robin? Sweetheart?" she called out softly just in case he'd dozed off, not wanting to startle him. Still no response. When she got close enough to see him and saw that he wasn't sleeping, she got another mother's feeling. Something was wrong.

She went close and sat next to him, leaning her back against the tree like his. "Sweetheart? Are you alright?" she asked quietly. Robin just shrugged his shoulders, not looking at her. She put her arm around him and pulled close to him. "Wanna talk?" He just shrugged again. "Don't you like the new house?" she asked, feeling the need to start narrowing down the possibilities.

Robin nodded. "Yeah, I do," he replied somberly.

"Don't you like your room? You can have any one you want."

Robin set his volume of Kipling's *Kim* aside and pulled his knees up to his chest and she knew he was closing her off.

"Please, sweetheart, talk to me. We've always been best friends; remember *you and me against the world?*"

The boy nodded, and then said without looking up at her. "Why did my dad have to die?"

"Oh, sweetheart!" Renee said ruefully, pulling him closer to her and wanting to cry, ever so much more for him than for herself. "Is that it?" His question caught her off guard and she wasn't sure where it was coming from, then a flash thought crossed her mind. *George! Was this somehow triggered by George coming into their lives and everything happening so quickly, their meeting and falling in love, the marriage and the move into one big house together? It had to have had some repercussions for Robin that she wasn't aware of.* And she immediately felt guilty for not seeing it coming or understanding. George and Robin had seemed to get along so well, right from the beginning.

"If I ask you a question, will you tell me the truth?" she asked gingerly, not wanting to rock the boat any more than she obviously already had. Robin hesitated, then nodded.

"Is this about George?" she fished.

The boy shrugged and nodded.

"But I thought you liked George."

The boy nodded again and said, "I do, a lot...he's great."

"So what is it? Please tell me, sweetheart." The boy let his head drop lower. She could see the thin line of water run down one side of his face.

"I heard him on the phone with Drake at college this morning." Then he hesitated.

Renee jumped in. "Did he say something that hurt your feelings?"

Robin shook his head. "No. It was just that...they're so close, laughing and making fun of each other...and all the kids at school have real fathers, even the divorced ones get their weekends and holiday time and I...I...don't have anyone," he said and put his head down on his knees.

Renee's heart broke into pieces for her son. Had she been selfish in depriving him of a father in his life? Had she made the wrong decisions even though she thought she was doing the right thing? She pulled him even closer to her, tears running down her own face for having let her son down even though she'd tried her best.

"Robin, I'm so sorry."

# INSIDE A HAUNTED MIND

---

## PREFACE

### A Journal Found

By way of introduction, I feel I should explain how the enclosed text came into my possession. I've also included a few additional notes which explain what was necessary to bring it to completion. First, I am an accountant by trade and training, but I've been a junk hound for most of my adult life having spent years rummaging through flea markets, garage sales and junk shops as a means of release from the tedium of the numbers I've dealt with for more than twenty-five years. What I look for mostly are pieces of antique jewelry, china, pottery and glass, small items that can be easily placed in the house or resold on eBay. It was during one of these events that I came across the enclosed document. The following are the particulars.

I was on a weekend treasure hunt in northeastern Pennsylvania in the fall of 2004 to attend a "Giant Flea Market," not looking for anything in particular, but nevertheless hopeful of coming across the ever elusive "flea market find." By midday, I had found a Carltonware pot, an early Christian Dior brooch and a Mdina Maltese paperweight from 1934 (hallmarked and dated on the bottom). The Mdina paperweight was in a box lot, which I rarely have any interest in, but it was clear that no one recognized the value of it, so I bought the whole thing knowing the paperweight alone was worth no less than fifty or seventy-five dollars. The box itself was approximately two feet long, two feet deep, one and a half feet wide and had the name of an egg company printed on the sides. The other items in the box included a few tattered men's garments, some dishes and other commonplace household odds and ends, but since I was only interested in the paperweight, I didn't pay much attention to the other items until I got home later that afternoon and unpacked the box.

When I went through the remainder of its contents, I discovered the manuscript at the bottom of the box tied with twine and wrapped in a dusty, regional New York State newspaper dated June 2002. The pages it contained were handwritten in blue and black ink. Not quite as big as an average telephone book nor as heavy, it was bound by what appeared to be the remains of a three-hole binder notebook of the kind typically used by college students a decade or so ago, but with the binding clasps removed from the inside.

Ordinarily, I have no interest in documents and this one was certainly not old, but for the sake of thoroughness, I unwrapped the parcel and thumbed through the contents thinking I might come across some rare stamps or postcards. One really never knows what one may find, even in the most unlikely of places. What I found, however, were not old postcards or stamps, but what appeared, at first glance, to be a journal...but not just any journal. I was riveted from the very first words on the opening page, and took it out on my front porch to read the entire document. I became so consumed by what it contained that it wasn't until I had finished the entire volume well on into the night (or more accurately, close to the next morning), that I realized I was drenched in my own sweat, my hands having given in to a slight tremble by what just simply could not be real. I didn't sleep at all that night and had only uneasy sleep for several nights after.

It was during one of those nights of uneasy sleep that I finally realized what I had to do. I had to go public with it. The following text is the result. But before continuing, there are a few things the reader should understand. First, for the sake of my respect for humanity and avoidance of any legal trouble, my conscience has required me to change the names of people and places named in the original document, along with some minor details regarding a number of specific events in order to maintain the privacy of those involved, both dead and alive. Above all considerations, it's important that their memories, as well as their families, are protected. The last thing I would want to result by doing what I have done here would be for droves of reporters, paranormal investigators or wannabe ghouls to converge on the parties involved or their loved ones. It has always been a standard of my life that my conscience takes precedence over the lure of dollars so not even America's Mysteries, the Sci-Fi Channel, or Oprah Winfrey herself, could ever make me divulge the true details.

Secondly, I've had to restructure the text to make it readable to the average person in areas of dialogue, formatting, paragraphing, spelling, etc. I did this with the indispensable aid of a professional editor to whom I will forever be indebted for his help in bringing the text to life. In its original form, each smaller notebook contained in the larger manuscript seemed to have been written as one long "stream of consciousness" type of work over a short period of time and was evident throughout that, at the time of its writing, the writer did not intend the thoughts, ideas and events contained therein to be made available for public consumption. Thus, the reformatting, as well as the other editorial actions, was absolutely necessary to bring the manuscript to its current state.

The original text also contained numerous scratch outs, illegible words (giving the impression that they were written in a state of extreme haste) and, in places, was marred to a blur by numerous large water stains. As such, certain substitutions were required to maintain both the flow of the dialogue and the continuity of the story, but please be advised that these substitutions were made only where absolutely necessary to the completion of the project, with careful attention and every effort made to retain the integrity of the original. I have also divided the text into chapters with titles that seemed appropriate to the content. Then, to further highlight the complexity of emotions portrayed in the original text, I have added selected quotations culled from both contemporary and historical sources to these chapter headings (as well as the opening and closing pages) as they would be reflected from my point of view, rather than that of the participants themselves. In the end, I can only say that I have already drawn my own conclusions about the content of the journal. Now it is up to the individual reader to decide for themselves but, upon my advice, hopefully not at night and especially not alone.

Daniel Vincent Carruthers, C.P.A.
Montclair, New Jersey
May 2005

# BOOK ONE

## THE PRECIPICE

*All day, staring at the ceiling*
*Making friends with shadows on my walls*
*All night, hearing voices telling*
*That I should get some sleep*
*Because tomorrow may be good for something*
*Hold on,*
*Feeling like I'm heading for a. . . breakdown*
*And I don't know why*
*But I'm not crazy, I'm just a little unwell*
*I know, right now you can't tell*
*But stay awhile and maybe then you'll see*
*A different side of me*
*I'm not crazy, I'm just a little impaired*
*I know, right now you don't care*
*But soon enough, you're gonna think of me*
*And how I used to be . . . me.*

*Unwell*--Rob Thomas

# CHAPTER 1

## Unwell

*". . .then black despair. The shadow of a starless night was thrown over the world in which I moved alone."*

-Percy Bysshe Shelley,
Early 19th Century Romantic Poet &
husband of Mary Shelley, author of "Frankenstein," from
*The Revolt of Islam-Dedication* (st.6)

January 2002

God, I'm so afraid! I can hardly breathe. I don't know what to do anymore or where to turn for help, or even if there can be any help for me. Could there be anyone out there who knows fear the way I do? Are they still alive? If they are, they'll know the hell I've lived in these past months, every day, every second and at this very moment as I struggle to hold my pen straight to keep it from shaking out of control, someone to know what it's like to live with the kind of relentless panic that makes me want to run and hide, knowing full well there is nowhere to run, nowhere to hide. But that would be incredibly selfish, wouldn't it? Inhuman, really. My conscience would never let me wish this even on my worst enemy. Martin is the closest thing I have to someone who might understand, but I've kept so much from him to try and protect him. Then what little he does know, he doesn't remember. I guess that's for the best. It's all just like one long nightmare for him, fading day by day as he gets better, and poor Jenny, the brief glimpse of it that she saw almost sent her over the edge. I could never burden her life any further with this. She's done so much for Martin already. It would be unconscionable, beyond unforgivable.

I've been cursed by so many things, not the least being an unfailing ability to hold everything tightly inside myself. It's served me well lately, though. Up 'til now, I've managed to protect those around me that I hold so close, even at the cost of my own sanity. I'm sweating so hard right now. It's running down the back of my neck, dripping down my forehead, running into my eyes, stinging them, mixing with my own shameful tears as they run down my face, droplets of myself splashing the page as I try to get this all down, or are they tears? I just don't know anymore. I don't know who I am, or even if I am. I'm so cold, chills of an invisible current from somewhere beyond myself running over my flesh making the hair stand up on my arms, and my nerves…twitching through my brain as this unholy current works its way down through every inch of my being making the nerve endings snap like tiny light bulbs bursting from a sudden surge of high voltage electricity. It's like this all the time and has been for so long that I have to keep my bowels on constant guard, afraid they'll get away from me like a small child in the night, terrified of the unknown thing in the bottom of the closet, or the monster under the bed that may not stay there…but I'm not a child. I'm an adult, and for me, the thing won't go away when the sun comes up. It'll be waiting for me, waiting until I'm dead, and possibly even beyond.

I've been such a fool, taken so much for granted. I just want to be normal again, or as normal as I ever was. I watch people on the street, soccer moms, businessmen, teenagers, little old ladies with blue hair, and find myself wishing more than anything that I was one of them…any of them…anyone but myself. I'm jealous of what they don't know. In their everyday lives they have the luxury of ordinary kinds of fear, car wrecks, plane crashes…disease. They routinely think that

the worst they have to fear is death, but that's not true.
There's more. I know…much more. God! I feel so
abandoned…so alone, clinging to my gun…just in case.

I used to think that grief was the worst of all human
emotions, back in the days when I thought it would swallow
me whole. I know better now. At least my father is safe and
at peace, but for me, having managed to come this far, I
realize I was so very deadly wrong. Fear is the cruelest feeling
in the human vocabulary of emotions. It's the cancer of the
mind, of the soul, black cells multiplying by the thousands
inside me every day, gnawing away at what's left of whatever
made me feel like I was a man. I can feel them again now,
thick black clots breaking off inside me, dissolving in my
blood, running through my veins, seeping from my pores,
choking me with that awful smell, the smell of my own fear.

From the first time I saw that house, I should've known.
Some primal instinct inside tried to warn me, but I didn't
listen. Maybe somewhere in the back of my mind, I knew all
the time it would come to a showdown between us. It was
going to be either it or me, and as I sit here wallowing in my
own sweat, it looks like it, or my gun, will win. I'm so tired of
living with an unknown that takes such delight in having
shown its ugliness to me, wanting me to know it as if we were
lovers discovering each other's bodies for the first time,
making me feel dirty and…violated as if it were raping my
sanity and my humanity. I think I must feel fear as only the
rarest of human beings can. I pity them…and myself for
having discovered an evil more base than any human being
should ever have to face…and letting it beat me, making me a
prisoner in my own mind, alone with the knowledge of things
that transcend the human soul and the monstrous acts
committed by men who create them.

It knows I'm writing about it. The hair on the back of
my neck just stood up. It's here again, toying with me. I can't
stop my teeth from clattering no matter how tightly I clench
my jaw. I'm not sure what to do right now. Oddly enough,
when I know it's here, I still try to convince myself that it's

not real, that somehow I've found myself in some cosmic 'reality TV' episode of *The Twilight Zone* or *The Outer Limits,* but in the darkest spaces of everything that still makes me human, I know I'm not. This is no movie. It's all too horribly real. There'll no safe haven when the lights come up. For me, there'll only be the cold reality of mind-bending, body-numbing fear; fear for my immortal soul. I have to stop here, close my eyes and wait until it goes away—if it goes away. It tends to come and go these days. I don't think it has what it wants yet, or I wouldn't be here to write this.

❊ ❊ ❊

It's gone away again…for now, but it's left me drifting back to the idea of the soul. Since this all began, I've realized that most people go through their daily lives completely unaware. They never consider things such as the human soul, theirs or anyone else's for that matter. Even the most devout have only the most abstract concepts of it, as if it were a wisp of air, ethereal and fleeting. I don't think I particularly blame them. I've come to believe that their fanciful ideas are simply a result of the limitations of our mortal selves, our bodily beings, but at least that's something, and they're safe. I'm not. After all, not everyone has had the privilege of crossing the barriers between life and death, heaven and hell, the way I have. Lucky me!

Others don't believe in the human soul at all. Having had my own faith run through the meat grinder by the randomness of life on earth, I used to be one of those, but I'm a true believer now. I know it exists. I live every day in fear for my soul and the souls of those I love because I know now what souls can become. I've seen them, heard their voices. I've felt their touch on my skin, but it's even worse than that…much worse, because not all of them are harmless or good. Casper, the friendly ghost, yeah right! I'd laugh if I weren't so afraid I'd cry again and I can't afford to break down right now. But make no mistake there are those that are here for no other reason than to hurt us. Malignant and rotted, they thrive on the evil they create as they seek to consume the souls of others and make them suffer. They delight in the suffering of others because it sustains them. My skin crawls even to write about it. Then when I feel it near me and can smell its breath as I have for months now, constantly hammering at my senses, I have to doubt every sound, every movement, every thought and perception. It's even forced me to doubt my own sanity because it's easier to think that I've gone stark raving mad than to believe what I know to be true: that evil exists right beside us every day, surrounding us, waiting patiently in the cold, dark recesses of the human soul. Even more than that, what happens when evil bound in human form is released from the body? What then? God help me, I know the answer now. I need another drink. I still have to exist, at least for now, even if I'm reduced to clinging to the barest, most elemental animal instinct in nature to sustain me—the will to survive.

I'm calmer now and have some sensibility about me. With a clear head, I still can't help but try to think it through, get my head around it all as best as I can. No matter what I do, I keep coming back to the same thing—the fear. Fear has got to be the evil soul's strongest weapon, the way it can use it against you, driving you beyond all rationality. Then when you've become consumed by it body and soul, you realize, as I did at first, that there are really only two options of escape for someone in its grip…like I am right now. Suicide, or true, drooling, howling insanity.

Once you've come that far and your mind and spirit are bent so far out of shape from your ordinary reality that you don't even recognize yourself, it becomes clear how someone living under the pressure of such an unrelenting fear can be forced to choose between the two. I've had time to reflect on the suffocating feeling of a trapped animal it creates, understanding it like no one else. I guess that's why I'm writing this, grasping wildly in the dark for a third option that may offer some hope for my survival, even if only for a little while. It's my pressure valve opening in one last desperate bid to keep myself from the other two.

I need to put this down, what I've felt, seen, what I've done and why…or lose my mind. It's my only focus, my only concentration. Whether it's ever read by anyone else is unimportant. I just want to keep from putting my gun in my mouth or having the state take me away in a straightjacket. I'm not sure which would be worse, but I don't know how much longer I can stand this. The way I feel right now, I know it can't be long, maybe only weeks, possibly only days. Then I worry about what would happen to Martin. The thought of him alone and at its mercy terrifies me, even more than it does for myself. I just know one thing. I will not give up his soul…or mine…not without a fight. If I have to die, I'll die fighting in a way that'll deprive it of its final victory over me. If it goes that way, I just pray that it'll be in a state of grace. I have to believe that even if I have to do us both, God'll understand that we died a good death and finally embrace me in a blanket of light, because I've learned in these last few months that there are worse things than death. I've seen the face of it and know its true nature. Worst of all, I know it's here and it's coming for me again, for both of us, coming back to get whatever it is that it wants, so time is not on my side. I'm having another panic attack. I have to put my head down for a while. I'll come back to this when I wake up—assuming I do wake up.

Morning is here and I guess I managed to sleep a little. It's hard to tell sometimes. I may have just been lying there in a narcotic- and alcohol-induced trance, afraid to let go. I can't really tell, but I can see the light of the winter sun through the window, feel its warmth on my face, so I guess I'm must still be alive. It doesn't seem to show itself in the mornings, small miracles I guess. Sleep for me these days is like a double-edged sword. I'm afraid to go to sleep thinking I might not ever wake up again; then I'm afraid of waking up to find that nothing has changed. But let me get back to where I left off in the best way I know how.

I'm going to have to take this one step at a time. My mind has been so fractured from months of struggling with a knowledge that no human should ever be forced to comprehend that the focus a thorough, methodical approach would afford is all I can think of to get it down before it's too late. I suppose I should start with who I am, how I got to this place and how I became its prisoner. Maybe if I put it all down and go over it again in writing, I'll find something I've missed, something I failed to do when I tried to destroy it, but then…can one ever really destroy evil?

Maybe I'll see something in my life to this point that has made me the target I've become. No matter what the end result, it'll help me to collect myself, even if only temporarily, and allow me to breathe for a while, to relive what good memories I have, brief moments of love and freedom, pride and accomplishment, "Putting my effects in order," so to speak. It can help remind me of times before the darkness overcame my life and my mind making me break into cold sweats when there's a creak in the floorboards thinking that it's coming for me, tremble when there's a noise in the house thinking that it's beside me, and shake uncontrollably when the wind is at the windows thinking I can hear it call my name.

Evil is the most insidious creature imaginable because it can live forever. It has all the patience it needs to lie in wait until it's ready to strike, and it always strikes when its prey is at its weakest and most vulnerable to its tricks. It seems only now, in hindsight, that the traumas and tragedies of everyday life that I always took for granted as the worst that could happen to me seem so insignificant. Unfortunately, it's only now that I've felt the breath of the foulest, most godless evil imaginable on the back of my neck that I realize it but, of course, now it's too late.

❋ ❋ ❋

My name is Terrence Arthur Chagford and I'm the Chief of Police of Jennisburg, New York, a quiet, unassuming little burg. Just another one of those small upstate towns of under a thousand people named after its founder back in seventeen hundred and something, famous for nothing more than its maple syrup, apples, peaches and cows. I was born here forty-one years ago to very loving parents. My mother, God love her, is a psychiatric nurse at the hospital about ten miles over in the nearest large town of Henriston, just about to retire, and not a moment too soon if you ask me.

My father was a state police officer, a good man and a great cop, not one of those miscreants with a gun and a badge who get off on bullying people under color of law just because they can. He always said that those kinds of cops were only trying to make up for their own personal deficiencies and the job was the only thing that made them feel that they had any power; the whole big gun-little dick sort of theory. It was always, "To Protect and Serve," with Arthur Chagford, and do it with respect and a sense of dignity that let people know they were in good hands. He was a decent man who respected people and was respected by them for it. I remember him teaching me that from my earliest memories when we'd go fishing together on the river or hiking in the mountains. Even just walking down a street in town with him, people would stop to put their hands out for him to shake, smiling the kind of smile that can't be faked, no matter how hard one might try, genuine, real, warm. I can see it so clearly in my mind now. They would take his hand in theirs to shake it then put their other hand over top of his so that they were holding his hand in both of theirs. People just don't do that unless they think you're special. Their eyes would always shine as they looked into his, honest and unafraid, open and accepting. I always got the feeling that they felt he'd done them a good turn or had protected them in some way that they'd never forget.

That was my dad. I loved him very much. I guess I probably shouldn't use the past tense here because I still do, and I miss him terribly, even after all these years. Especially now. As I sit here I can't help but wonder what kind of man I might've become had he not been killed leaving me the half-formed human being that I am. Would this even be happening to me? *Focus, Terry, Focus.* I have to keep saying that to myself. I can feel it welling up inside me again, the panic, the anxiety. I can't let it get to me here or I'll never finish this. If I do, it'll paralyze me. I can't let that happen, not now that I've finally found the balls to do it. I've got to beat it down and move on.

❀ ❀ ❀

I was just a regular kid of the times, not particularly special in any obvious way. I ate peanut butter and jelly or bologna and cheese sandwiches on Wonder bread out of my Batman lunch box, watched Wonderama and Soupy Sales on a black and white TV. You know, that kind of kid, just bigger than most my age, a little chubby and kind of clumsy. It wasn't until high school that I seem to have surprised everyone, including myself, and became...not so ordinary anymore. It's what put me on the path I've stumbled down ever since. I call it "my metamorphosis." It seemed like, almost overnight, I wasn't chubby anymore or clumsy, or shy and backward. I also seemed to have found my voice and, to my utter amazement, people started to listen, my teachers, my friends, my parents. That was when my grades began to soar and what would later become my athletic gifts started becoming apparent. I remember when the track and field coach came to my house to speak to my parents about joining the team. He told them that my regular gym teacher had asked him to come and watch me in class to see if he thought he could develop my potential. I remember thinking to myself then, *What potential?*

The whole thing mystified me so I just did what they told me, pleased for the attention. Looking back now, I can't shake the idea that it left me with an insatiable hunger for accomplishment, craving approval at every turn, while at the same time setting me up for the feelings of failure that would follow my life with an all too alarming consistency. I ended up graduating high school with the second highest grades in my class. "Bringing up the rear," I call it. I still got both academic and athletic scholarships, though, and decided on the State University at Albany. I guess I could have gone anywhere. I had plenty of offers, but I wanted to stay as close to my mother as I could, for both our sakes. It was a bad time then. It would have been for anyone who'd lost someone they loved so suddenly and so senselessly.

The unimaginable had found its way to our door in the form of two uniformed state troopers. My father had been killed in a high speed car chase, and my mother needed me, so I wanted…needed to stay close to home. We needed each other, really. I don't think either of us ever really recovered from it. People don't recover from things like that. It just lives inside you in a little box, opening up every now and again to remind you that it'll hurt you until the day you die. Time seemed to have stood still so long for me then, like my head was encased in concrete. Months went by before I realized I was still alive and that it was real, not just a bad dream. I have my mother to thank for bringing me out of it…by force, her hands pushing me out of the front door when the day came for me to leave, pulling me by my arm to the bus that would take me to Albany.

"I don't want to go. Please, Ma, I'm not ready yet…don't make me go!" I begged, sobbing like a child half my age. "I'm afraid!"

"You have to do this, Terry. You're all I have now and he wants so much for you to make something of yourself. It's his dream for you. Do it for me…and for him. He loves you so much, Terry. Get on that bus!" she cried as pushed me up the steps. It wasn't until I looked out of the window as the bus was pulling away that it dawned on me. She wasn't able to speak of him in the past tense, yet...

❄ ❄ ❄

I must have drifted off somewhere for a while. I don't remember writing that last bit. But that's just the way it happened. I'm soaking wet now, all down the front of my shirt. I have to change into dry clothes and throw some cold water on my face if I'm going to continue. I don't even know what time it is. Time just seems to shift under my feet, like an undertow in a storm, eroding reality into something I no longer recognize. Maybe I took one pill too many. All I know is that it's still light out; I need to get a grip on myself and keep anyone else from knowing what's been going on. Martin should be coming down soon anyway. I can't let him see me this way.

❄ ❄ ❄

Martin has gone to bed early. He does almost every night. He's still on the mend, so by 9:00 P.M. he's worn out by the day's struggles. It was a quiet day in town, and even quieter yet since I got home—alarmingly quiet. It sounds like what I imagine a tightly wound rubber band must sound like right before it snaps in your face. I'm going to try and get as much done as I can tonight because no one knows better than I do the potential for unexpected events that tomorrow may bring. My head is still clear. I can thank the cold weather for that, nothing like a bracingly cold wind to pull you out of a haze, substance induced or otherwise. I guess I'll pick up with my years at school. That seems to be the time when I was closest to reaching my goals, but even then, it all came crashing down around my head. Anyway...once I'd come out of the shock my father's death, the only thing left for me to do was to try to be the best that I could to make him proud of me. I chose Criminal Justice as my major in his honor. Although, looking back now, maybe it was more to see if I could be him, replacing his loss with myself.

❊ ❊ ❊

My first year away was a hard road to acceptance, alternately rocky and pocked with deep trenches of blackness that forced me to take to my bed every few weeks, staying there with the lights off until it passed. After that, I decided that the only way I would survive would be to channel all my grief, anger and loneliness into school work and sports. I got that idea from a book I read on coping with grief. Sometimes I think that book saved my life, although for what it was saved, I'm still at loss to understand.

I kept as much of it from my mother as I could. She had her own grief to deal with. I felt guilty enough having to leave her alone, so the idea of making her cope with my grief on top of her own was unthinkable. Funny, sometimes, how one's love for others can block out whatever else they might be feeling. I guess that was the first time I felt like a 'protector.' It made me feel good. I found strength in it that helped me make it through, probably seeming to the outside world like an 'All American' success story, while on the inside being nothing more than a hollow, pointless, directionless, empty shell of not quite a man.

I did have my rewards during those years, though. As it turned out, my channeling exercises led me to being chosen for the 1980 Summer Olympics team for the pole vault and broad jump. My mother was so proud when she read it in the newspaper. I could hardly understand her through her tears when she called to tell me about the article. I didn't even know the final decisions had been made, but more importantly, it was the last time I heard or saw her cry. To me, that was my real accomplishment. It's not that she didn't cry when I wasn't around. I'm sure she did, and often. It's just that it made me feel that I'd given her at least one reason not to cry.

❋ ❋ ❋

I'm drifting again, losing time, like I'm not really here but somehow hovering above my own life, watching it but completely powerless to change it. It's strange how the past can come back to you and seem so vividly alive when the present seems so hopeless and the future seems non-existent. I saw the same thing happen to Grace when we had our 'little talk.' Now I know how she felt. I can empathize with the wisdom of her age, but I'll get to that later. If I can get that far. For now, I'd better move on, back to the Olympics.

❋ ❋ ❋

It was 1980 and the world was in a particularly tense state of self-induced political distress. The Cold War was still arctic, even though the threat of nuclear war had taken a back seat. Mexican stand-offs, posturing and boycotts were the current trend so participation by the United States and fifty other countries from the Moscow Olympiad ended up being withdrawn because of the Soviet invasion of Afghanistan. Do I have the best fucking luck in the world or what? You really gotta laugh sometimes because I was having an increasingly rare good spell then. I even had the nerve to dare and think I could win, but fate apparently had other ideas. I did eventually end up going to Los Angeles with the team in '84, but by then I was older, not in as good a shape and suffering one of the blackest spells I'd had up to that point. I managed to rally for a little while right before the events, but the coach and I both knew it was too late.

Ironically, I came back home to a hero's welcome for my two bronze medals. Go figure, third place. Like I said, it's the story of my sad fucking life to 'bring up the rear.' No Wheaties box covers for me. Endorsements went to superstars and I was only…well…an 'also ran' or a 'has been' or a changeling of something in-between the two, and in events nobody really cared about anyway. After that I decided that I wouldn't try again. Sports achievements were a useless accomplishment. So many things felt useless to me after that. I just said, "Fuck it!" and gave up. The black spells, although less frequent from then on, became longer in duration. But when they did come, they were more like 'black holes' than 'black spells.' They got so bad sometimes that I couldn't really tell if they would ever end, much less when. The only positive thing I can say about that time was that, by then, I'd at least learned how to hide them from almost everyone, except my mother. We didn't talk about it for a long time, but I know she knew. Mothers always do—particularly mine.

With my Los Angeles 'triumph' behind me, I managed to summon up the last shred of what my mother, in trying to dissuade me, called my "… youthful idealism and enthusiasm." But, stubborn as I've been all my life, I held fast and fierce to the feeling that I could still make myself useful in some way. It seemed like it was all I had left to keep me breathing. I figured that if I made some real impact on other people's lives, it might make me a worthwhile human being instead of the walking, breathing carcass I'd become. If I couldn't be happy for myself, I had to at least offer myself up and do the best I could for others, thinking that maybe their lives might fare a little better through me so that the dwindling core of goodness I still felt inside wouldn't be completely wasted. I'd hoped I might find some salvation in that, by being a 'protector' again.

My father never wanted me to be a trooper like he was. He wanted better for me as any parent would, so I tried to get into the FBI. The upshot of that was—that's right, you guessed it—they didn't want me. Who knows, maybe my psychological exam gave them a glimpse of what was to come. Whatever it was, the 'other' federal police didn't seem to have a problem with it, so there I was, an 'also ran' yet again. You've really got to laugh at it all. I'm nothing if not consistent. Nevertheless, the ATF gave me confidence again, and a purpose, and a reason to live. Little did I or anyone else at the time know, but in those next few years, my 'quiet' agency was just about to heat up to white hot and, not least of all, for me, nothing would ever be the same again because of it.

❋ ❋ ❋

David Koresh and his Branch Davidians had created a compound of allegedly 'dangerous subversives' in a place called Waco, Texas. It was said that they had an arsenal of weapons in a compound there and were hurting children. The shameful fiasco that later became euphemistically known as "The Waco Incident" was approaching its deadly and disastrous conclusion while the rest of the south was ablaze with flames from the burning of black churches being set by one or more racist lunatics on a rampage of hate. True to form, I wasn't assigned to that primary Waco project, thank God, but pulled what was thought to be at the time, a lower priority assignment, investigating the burning of the churches.

I still don't understand the logic there. Sketchy allegations of guns and white parents supposedly hurting their children justified the government burning and killing them all, but the random burning out of decent, hardworking, churchgoing people on a routine basis by a lunatic fringe hardly made a ripple, left to back page news and tail end stories. It's a funny thing about 'threats' in a multi-media world, either real or imagined. They can become so subjective and prime for being worked out of all reality by 'spin doctors' who spend their lives turning truth into lies and lies into truth to the point where no one can tell the difference anymore. I guess, in some minds, the life of a little white child is still more valuable than that of a little black one, so no one ever really heard about the little black one. Did they? Gotta love it don'tcha? Jeeze, I just got such a bitter taste in my mouth.

I'm gonna get a drink to wash it out before it gets too comfortable in there.

Anyway…my team and I traveled throughout the south for months, always seeming to be one step behind the arsonists. My men were good men, but the frustration we were all feeling kept building until it had us all at the boiling point. Then, one night while we were staying in a tiny town in southwestern Tennessee not far from Memphis, they struck right under our noses. Less than five miles away from where we had stopped for the night, another church was torched. For the first time, we were on the spot and leapt on it with all we had. That night, and the crushing baggage I'd carry away from it, would change my life forever…again.

As we approached the site, the dark night sky was already glowing with the surreal light of the white clapboard church, simple and small, being devoured by flames like a legion of demons spewing forth from hell, dancing gaily at their newfound freedom. But even worse than the sight of it were the sounds. When I got out of the car, all I could hear were voices, shouting, screaming to us that there were people still in there. God, it still hurts me so badly I can't breathe. Each time I think of it my heart bleeds out into a river of sorrow, flowing from a half-healed wound of guilt and loss; tearing it open daily so that it can continue to live inside me.

There was a young woman named Cordelia Weston, a victim of domestic abuse, and her eight-year-old daughter, Angelica, still in the burning building. They'd been left homeless and were living there in a few unused rooms upstairs in exchange for maintenance work. They were trapped upstairs in the back when the fire was set underneath them. Just as my men and I approached the action, I could see the woman being carried out by one of the few local firefighters who'd arrived not long before we did. They'd found her after she'd managed to make her way as far as the stairs. Blinded by smoke and covered with soot, she was screaming and crying with the kind of unrestrained abandon that could only mean one thing—her child was still in there.

As long as I live, I will never…never forget the pleading sound of her voice, her anguished, shrill cries. "My baby! My baby! Somebody, please save my baby!" she screamed, smoke streaming from her singed hair and blackened nightgown as she fought her rescuer to get back into the blazing building.

That poor woman. It seems that when the fire broke out, the little girl ran and hid out of…fear. Without even giving myself a second to think, I did the one thing I had been so rigorously trained not to do, but what I knew my father would have done. I ran in. I could hear my men shouting at me from behind as they followed with our equipment, but I was too fast. Fueled with an eruption of energy I didn't know I still had, I flew through that door. When I got to the bottom of the stairs, I heard the little girl's voice crying with a terror she should've never had to know. "Mama! Mama!" Using muscles I'd forgotten I had for ten years, I shot up the stairs, taking them three at a time until I was more than halfway up. The last thing I remember was getting the briefest glimpse of her frightened little face illuminated by the flames that had imprisoned her as she hid in the back of the linen closet, seeing the helpless panic in her eyes as she saw me. I reached out my hand out to her. Just as I opened my mouth to call to her, "I'm coming, baby," I felt the burning rafter come crashing down on me, catching me between my neck and shoulder, the stairs giving way beneath my feet and that horrible dreamlike feeling of falling further and further into darkness with the certain knowledge that I'd failed her, failed us both.

When I woke up in the hospital, the little girl was dead. As I laid there with my broken right collarbone, right hand and forearm, broken left ankle and foot, fractured right knee and scattered spots of second and third degree burns all over my upper body and legs, with a concussion thrown in for good measure, I wished I had died in there with her. But it wouldn't be that easy for me. I was doomed to live the rest of my life with the big L on my forehead . . . branded forever . . . *Loser!*

I'll always believe in my heart that her death was my fault. I can't get away from it. I should have done more, run faster, been...better. That poor little girl. Her death has burned a cavernous, bottomless pit in my soul that will last until the day I die. I relive it at least once every day, usually at night when I'm alone and can hear the echoes of her tiny voice crying out, over and over, "Mama, Mama." I couldn't sleep in the days that followed, dreaming that I could still see the terror in her eyes, beckoning me to save her, pleading. That makes two now. My father's death was the first. He did what he thought was best to feed us, keep a roof over our heads and live like a man of honor the only way he knew how, and he died because of it. I wanted so much to be like him. Now there was Angelica. Her death was my own personal failure, an everlasting mark of inadequacy on my conscience. My shirt is wet again. My head hurts...and my eyes, but I've got to get past this tonight.

Cordelia Weston came to the hospital a few days after the funeral. She was a thin, frail-looking woman of no more than thirty-five with smooth cocoa skin, spotted in places by scorch marks left by the spitting sparks. She wore a black turban to cover the places where the fire had burned her hair to the scalp. Her face was a portrait of blinding grief and pointless, endless loss; a portrait that I knew all too well. My mother wore it for years after my father was killed. I still wear it myself when no one is around. She brought me flowers and a school picture of Angelica, a pretty, bright eyed, smiling little girl with dark skin, pigtails and brightly colored barrettes. As I looked at it, I knew that her senseless loss, the waste of her human goodness, had broken my spirit in ways that the rafter could never have broken my body.

"I want to...thank you...for trying to save...my baby," she said haltingly with a light southern accent, taking my hand as she fought back tears through eyes nearly swollen shut from days of them, "...and tell you...how very sorry I am that you got hurt so badly tryin'. You're a very brave man, Mr. Chagford. I will never forget you." The unselfishness of her words and the kindness in her voice shattered whatever was left of my already brittle composure. This woman who had lost the most precious gift life had to give her had the presence of mind and generosity of heart to come see me, even though I'd failed. I didn't know what I could say to her that would give her any peace.

"I will hold her smile in my heart until the day I die, Mrs. Weston. I promise," I said, my throat sore and swollen from the smoke and the heat, my voice little more than a groaning whisper. I can still feel the soft pressure of her hand on mine, her warm tears on my skin as she held me to her. I had to be sedated after she left, but I've kept that promise to this day...unflinchingly, unfailingly every day. That was when I first started drinking. It offered me only the slightest relief from the pain, but it allowed me to sleep some. When you're desperate, you have to take what you can get.

The pill-taking thing has been more gradual, in cases of extreme pain. I've only begun taking them regularly in the last few months, on and off mostly, but more and more since the first time it came after me. I'm sure it loves when I'm in pain and I've got more than enough to feed its hunger. Maybe that's why it's waited for me. I know it's not a new evil. It's been around for a while, at least a hundred years, but it could be older. It had to come from somewhere before this...had to learn its tricks somewhere.

An analyst told me once that my drinking and taking pills "isn't the answer," but when I asked him what the answer was, what do you think he said? "I don't have any answers," while charging me a hundred dollars an hour for his sage advice, the thieving son of a bitch. I could've got that damn advice from Oprah on TV...for free. "Then don't mother fucking tell me my way isn't the answer unless you have something better to offer to replace it. I'm in pain, you fucking asshole, so if you don't have any goddamn answers what the hell do I need you for? Booze and pills are cheaper...and at least they do the job without taking Caribbean vacations on my hard-earned money, jerk off! " is what I told him in return, kicking the chair over as I stomped out of his priggish, over-decorated office, slamming the door behind me.

I'm going to put my head in my hands and sob now for a while. The wound is open again and it's...killing me. I need a pill and a drink, too. I'll pick up where I left off when I can, when I'm feeling better, maybe later on tonight. What little sleep I've been getting lately hasn't been serving me well, hardly at all really. I can't put my head down or I'll lose track again. I can't afford to lose any time just in case it comes back tonight. I've started to think that it's trying to wear me down to the point that when I do sleep, it'll be unshakable so that it can go after Martin and I won't be there to protect him. The hourglass never stops running for me and I've got to keep an ever watchful eye out for signs. It's the only plan I have.

❄ ❄ ❄

I'm better now. I've taken my pills and had a good, long drink. I stood out in the cold for a while without my coat. It revived me some, so I guess I'd better get on with this before my head gets too heavy and my eyes get too clouded to write.

❄ ❄ ❄

I was in the hospital for a few weeks before they released me to my own devices, such as they were, with my disability and pension still intact, even though what I did broke the rules. There I was, thirty-five years old and out of a job. They said my injuries were too severe to expect a full duty recovery because I'd never be able to run as fast, lift as much or move as quickly as the job required. They were right, I couldn't. Not without enormous effort and grimacing discomfort. But by then I'd lost my heart for it anyway, and the thought of being chained to a desk like a wounded animal in a cage, alone with my misery, was out of the question.

I must confess here, I've always wished we'd caught the rotten son-of-a-bitch responsible for that fire. Watching him fry for it would've at least given me some sense of justice. I think that was the first time in my life I'd ever truly had a taste of hate, the thick bile of festering injustice welling up from my guts into my throat, ready to spew itself out at those who turn their heads away from it. They did recover an unidentified male body in the ruins, burned beyond identification. I'll never know if it was the arsonist or just another poor soul seeking shelter unobserved for the night. Marginal lives can be that way. I've learned that, having become one of them myself, and ...*seeking out the poorer quarters where the ragged people go...* The worst part is that I'll never get my chance to spit on his grave, or even have the satisfaction of knowing that he's really dead. The way my luck runs, the dead man they found probably was just another lonely soul with nowhere else to go, like me, and the real murderer is still out there somewhere having a beer and laughing at me.

After a few more weeks of climbing the walls in some dump of a motel in Memphis, letting it all weigh on me, I looked over my resources, found that I enough money to feel as secure as I needed to be and decided to do the one truly selfish thing I think I've ever done in my life. I couldn't go home and face those I loved and respected looking at me, judging me, only to find me lacking or worse yet, pitying me like a three-legged dog with an ear torn off, so I ran away from it all...from my guilt...from my pain. It wasn't until later that I realized that there'd still be my own judgments to face when I looked at myself in the mirror and found myself lacking, seeing every day for myself what a three-legged dog that I was.

When I got to Europe I decided to try and drink it all away. It worried my mother half to death. That's something I'll always regret, but at the time, I was just too blinded by self-pity and vacancy of purpose to care anymore. I went to London first and drank their strong beer until it drained from my body of its own accord. I was a dirty, unshaven, ale-soaked wretch by the time I got to Paris a few months later, which is still little more than one big blur. I'm not really sure when or how I left Paris. All I know is that I landed in Spain where the booze was so cheap I could drown myself in it and almost did, literally. I was in a hospital there in Seville for a while. It seems I hadn't eaten in days and was floating in alcohol when I collapsed on the floor of some dive bar on the fringe of the city weighing twenty pounds lighter than when I had left home. ...*running scared, laying low, seeking out the poorer quarters where the ragged people go, looking for the places only they would know...* I remember the words from the old Simon and Garfunkel song played in my head as I went down, signaling me, as it has for years, that there was another black hole looming beyond the horizon, waiting to pull me in head first.

When I woke up a few days later, after having been sufficiently medicated, I got a message from the States. The doctor in Seville had contacted the U.S. Embassy in Madrid. They, in turn, contacted my mother through channels in New York City. She'd called the hospital and left word for me to contact her immediately.

When I was released a week later, my conscience got the better of me. I called her and was carefully and calmly informed in her most professionally practiced voice that she'd spoken to the Police Chief in Jennisburg, who just happened to be a buddy of my father's. They'd agreed that it would be best if I came home immediately to take a recently vacated officer's position. It seems that one of my old buddies from high school was leaving the force and moving to Florida to raise his family near his in-laws and they needed someone to fill the spot. It was agreed beforehand that, although my injuries may have disqualified me from federal duty, I would still be perfectly qualified for a small town job and it was hinted that I might move up quickly because of my experience and my father's connections. As much as she tried to contain it, the tone of her voice was one I'd heard only one other time before, after that knock on the door eighteen years earlier. Overwhelmed by guilt for having worried her so badly and leaving her alone again, I agreed to come home and take the job. By then guilt was like a Siamese twin attached to my side at all times, reminding me constantly that it had its needs, too. That's how I got here, who I was and who I am.

❀ ❀ ❀

I spent the next three years patrolling the eight-square-mile area that comprises my quiet, postcard picturesque little town of Jennisburg, looking out for under-age drinking, the smell of marijuana, graffiti and other sorts of vandalism, speeding and various traffic violations, not to mention the usual sundry domestic violence calls, but personally living in a self-imposed exile of the soul, a vacuum of the heart and a void of the…mind. Then, when Chief Oberson retired a couple of years later, the Mayor and Town Council, a number of whom were also friends of my father, appointed me to be the new Police Chief citing my long years of experience in high level law enforcement as my qualifications. I expected some resentment from the ranks but surprisingly enough, everyone was on board, which made me feel even more like a cripple than I already did. But since I was rapidly approaching forty and felt seventy when it got cold or rained, I wasn't in any position to make waves.

I took the job. I was long past anything resembling pride or dignity by then. But the real story, and the reason I'm writing this, was just about to begin. Even now, as I begin to think about what I'm about to say and how I'll ever say it, I can feel my stomach squeeze itself into a knot the size of a fist, beads of sweat already beginning to build on my forehead, upper lip and back of my neck getting ready to join hundreds of others like them for their trip down the rest of my body as I force myself to relive these last few months. The panic is already growing inside me, starting to make my hands shake. I'm weakening. I can't control it anymore. It's getting more difficult to write. I'm going to take half a pill and a good, long drink to steel myself. I cannot allow myself to falter here. The house is quiet now; I haven't felt it near me since yesterday, but I can't guarantee how long that'll last. I've got to begin in earnest. The time has come for me to put blinders on my fear, remember what it felt like to be a 'protector,' and let the devil have his due.

## Available Electronically and in Paperback

www.ingramcontent.com/pod-product-compliance
Lightning Source LLC
Chambersburg PA
CBHW070910030726
47504CB00005B/1534